IT DOES MEAN JACK

By
Carl Jordan

PublishAmerica
Baltimore

© 2011 by Carl Jordan
All rights reserved. No part of this book may be reproduced, stored in a retrieval system or transmitted in any form or by any means without the prior written permission of the publishers, except by a reviewer who may quote brief passages in a review to be printed in a newspaper, magazine or journal.

First printing

All characters in this book are fictitious, and any resemblance to real persons, living or dead, is coincidental.

PublishAmerica has allowed this work to remain exactly as the author intended, verbatim, without editorial input.

Hardcover 978-1-4560-8474-5
Softcover 978-1-4560-8473-8
PUBLISHED BY PUBLISHAMERICA, LLLP
www.publishamerica.com
Baltimore

Printed in the United States of America

To my children

Michael, Karen and Kenneth

THE WORLD DON'T LOOK GOOD

Jack woke up with a start. Instead of being in his cell in state prison, he was in his own bed, in his own house. His mind was foggy. *Maybe he had just had a bad dream.* No! it was real; his wife Gen, was not there his Ma was no longer with him he was alone why did everyone he loved have to die? He just felt completely alone.

Then he remembered, "Max Arnold," his attorney had won an appeal for him, and his father-in-law "John Parker" had put up a million dollar bail to get him released. Max had picked him up at prison and brought him to his house on the knoll. Where his wife and he had been so happy.

The last time he had seen his home he thought everything was completely perfect. He had a beautiful wife, they had just found out she was expecting, he had a great business and nothing could go wrong. Now things had completely changed.

"Go get you some rest; you've had a long hard day," Max had said.

Jack had the keys in his pocket. They were in the packet they turned over to him when he was released. He went in and flipped the switch and the lights came on. He didn't know who had the electricity turned on, or who had kept his lawn mowed but he was home and his home was so inviting and he was so tired he went to bed and slept sounder than he had for two years.

Later after he got his mind to working, he showered and put on a shirt and pants that were in his closet. He would have to wait until he got a charge on the battery in his shaver to shave. He found some coffee, brewed a pot and poured a cup. It was woody tasting because the grounds were two years old, but as bad as it was, it tasted better than the swill they had in prison.

Jack had been sentenced to 99 years for the murder of his wife, a crime that he knew he had not committed. He tried to think of who would want to kill his wife. That thought had been on his mind and he had wondered about it for over two years now. His mother had told him about a bill that John had collected for her from a man that was reputed to have had some underworld connections. But he didn't know who. John thought Gen may have caught someone in the stable doing mischief. But how could anyone find the culprit? Jack thought that the only way for him to stay out of prison was if a different jury would find him innocent. He just didn't know what to do.

Then he thought, *What would Gen do?*

"I'll call my Daddy," Gen would say.

He was reaching for the phone, when it rang. It was John.

"Welcome home," John said.

"I was about to call you and see if you knew what I should do now," said Jack.

"Just sit tight and I'll have Missie pick you up and take you to see Max. He can fill you in on where we stand."

After Jack hung up the phone, he drank another cup of that awful coffee, and shaved. Then Missie drove up. He came out the door, and Missie came running and grabbed him around the neck and kissed him on the lips.

"Oh it's good to see you without that glass between us!" She kissed him once more.

Jack was taken by surprise at Missie's enthusiasm.

"That was quite a greeting," said Jack.

"Didn't you like it?" Missie asked.

"It was okay," Jack said. But his answer wasn't what Missie was hoping for.

"Get in the car and I'll take you to the bank."

"I thought we were going to see Max," Jack said.

"His office is in the bank building, but let's stop and have some pancakes, you must be starved."

" I am, but I don't want to waste the time," Jack declined.

I wouldn't call any time we spend together a waste of time, Missie thought.

"Okay, Mister Party Pooper." She said.

She put on her pouting face and drove to the bank building.

THE YEAR OF 1950

Jim Adams and Mable Stewart were married in 1950. Jim did carpentry work and Mable was a waitress. Shortly after the wedding, Jim was drafted into the army. They were mostly separate for two years. After Jim's discharge from the military, he went back to being a carpenter, and Mable was still working in the restaurant, this time as a chef.

Jim had a dream to own his own contracting company. So he started going to college on the GI Bill, part-time. To make ends meet, Mable kept working. But Mable had a dream too. She wanted to be just a wife, and hopefully a wife and a mother.

When Jim got his degree in business, he contracted to build a large house and a stable for a banker. The home was on a large parcel of land the banker owned, just outside the town of Nixsonsville.

Next, Jim contracted to build a house for a couple on a lot the couple owned. The house was a three bedroom and two bath. But, when it was finished, the couple were unable to get financing because they were in the middle of a divorce. It presented Jim a problem, as he had several thousand dollars invested in the construction. To Mable, it presented an opportunity.

"Let's take the house for ourselves and live there," Mable said.

"You want to live next to a salvage yard?" Jim asked.

"Well I've met the man who owns the yard and he keeps the place looking nice. He's Sarah's husband. He don't come to church but Sarah does. It's an awfully nice lot too."

Jim gave the idea some thought, and agreed. A plan was worked out with the couple and Jim and Mable moved in. Their business continued to grow, not without its ups and downs, but it provided them a very comfortable living.

Phase one of Mable's ambitions was when she quit her job and became a full time home maker, and she loved every minute of it. She kept a very neat house, always paid close attention to her personal appearance, and cooked three meals a day. She went to church and was active in certain church activities, such as visiting shut-ins or the ill.

In 1960 Mable gave birth to a baby boy "Jack". He was perfect in every way. He was a handsome, healthy, dark haired boy, and Jim and Mable gloated over him. Jim had accomplished his ambitions and Mable her ambitions.

When they together thought about their future, it appeared to be happy and secure,...BUT!

THE YEAR OF 1970

The school bus stopped in front of Jack's house. Jack got off and ran in. Mable came from the kitchen, hugged him and said.

"How was your day honey?"

"Aw, it was alright, but we had to draw a picture of the insides of a frog."

"Did you do well?" asked Mable.

"I don't know, but Marian got sick and threw up, and then a lot the kids got sick".

"Did you get sick?" asked Mable.

"Heck no! I thought it was funny".

"Did the Marian see you laugh?"

"No, Mr. Chink was holding a paper towel under her mouth and took her out of the room, and Raymond said we ought to draw a picture of her puke and we both got tickled. Then when Mr. Chink came back, he said if anyone else was feeling sick they could wait in the hall until the class was over. Most of the girls went out, but Jerry was the only boy. Mr. Chink said that Jerry didn't look sick, and Jerry acted like he was going to throw up on Mr. Chink. Mr Chink jumped back and everybody in the room laughed".

"Oh that poor girl! She must have been terribly embarrassed," Mable said.

"I'm going out to ride my bike," said Jack. But before he could leave, Mable said,

"Not before you do your home work." Mable was always fair toward Jack and punishment never entered her mind. But when Mable said to do something he had learned that their was no sense arguing. Jack always felt that his parents were on his side in any circumstance. But the thing he was most quarrelsome about, and it was every Sunday, Jack never wanted to go to church. It was just one long hour that he hated. His only consolation was he got to sit next to his cousin Raymond during the service. Sometimes they could pass the time by playing hand games such as rock-paper-scissors, but they had to keep their hands below the pew so the preacher couldn't see. Their main objective each Sunday was they always tried to get out the front door before the preacher got there to shake everyone's hand. One Sunday after a successful try, they were laughing as they congratulated each other and an older woman scolded them saying,

"You boys stop that tom foolery!"

Mable heard it and and told the woman that if her boys needed correcting she would do it. After they got out of ear shot, Raymond mocked the way the woman sang. Jack started laughing and Mable was as quick to stop the mockery, as she was to stand up for Jack.

So when Mable said, "home work first", Jack knew it was home work first.

"Aw gee", said Jack, but he knew it was how it would be. He opened his note book and got out his work.

"It looks like rain anyway." Mable said.

Jack sprawled on the floor and began to write. He had a list of ten words he had to use in sentences. He only had to write five, because he and his cousin would each do half and they could copy the other half on the bus the next morning.

Suddenly there was a brilliant flash of lightning, with the loudest boom of thunder he had ever heard! Mable came running through the living room. She thought the lightning had hit the front of the house. She opened the front door and let out a blood curdling scream! Jim had just gotten out of his truck and had been struck by the lighting. He was lying on his back a few feet from his truck.

Sam Peebles, the owner of the shop next door, had heard the thunder and Mable's scream and came running. Mable was kneeling down by Jim and trying to revive him by patting him on the cheek. Sam got down beside her and told her to call an ambulance and he would try to revive Jim. Sam started giving him artificial respiration and was still trying when the ambulance arrived. The medics took over with their equipment, and told Mable that they would keep trying on the way to the hospital and took Jim away.

Jack was numb; he didn't realize the gravity of the situation. So he just stayed out of the way.

Mable was frantic, and called her sister "June" and told her what had happened. Sam wanted to help and said he would take Mable to the hospital.

"No" I've called my sister June and she's coming over," said Mable.

June was there in only minutes. She tried to comfort Mable and finally got enough information to make a rational decision on what to do. She drove Mable and Jack to the hospital and they were told that Jim had been declared dead. After what seemed to be an eternity of giving and getting information, they called a funeral home. Then another eternity of waiting, and finally getting them to accept the body, June drove them back home. June told Mable, she would come back in the morning and left.

The next morning June arrived about nine o'clock and Mable was glad to see her, because she had been unable to sleep at all. They went to the funeral home and made the arrangements for the funeral to be held the day after tomorrow. When they got home Mable called the reverend to ask him to officiate. He said he would and he came to Mable's house. Mable filled the reverend in on all the things he needed to know, but when she told him the funeral was to be held at the funeral home, he objected.

"A Christian service must be held in the church," he said. Then he quoted some obscure passage from the bible, to prove his point.

June butted in, "There are lots of scriptures you could quote, but this is what Mable wants and this is how it will be."

Mable was glad for June's intervention. Mable felt intimidated by the reverend, June did not.

News of Jim's death spread quickly. Some people came to see Mable and offered help that day, but not to many. The next day however a lot of people came by. Most of them brought food and many of them just wanted to offer their condolences. June pretty well took charge and would greet visitors and take what they brought, and more or less, usher people so they would not overwhelm Mable.

One woman came to the door and told June 'I'm here to see Mable,' and brushed right pass June. She went over to where Mable was and started talking.

"Oh my darling, I know just what you're going through. I've buried two husbands and when my last husband died, my mother died the same day. I've had so much trouble in my l ife".

June broke in and said, "I'm Mable's sister, have we met?"

"No," said the woman.

"Mable has a lot on her mind right now, I think it would be better if you didn't vent your problems on her".

"Well!" said the woman. Then she turned her back to June. But she didn't go back to Mable, and she left quietly.

After another exhausting day, when everyone had left, Mable was so tired, she was able to get a good nights rest. It was a good thing too because this was the day of the funeral. Mable was up early and found her kitchen in a mess from all the food people had brought and other clutter. She cleaned it up and fixed breakfast for herself and Jack.

The funeral home had a girl call Mable and tell her the funeral was at two, but they would send the family car to pick them up at one. At one o'clock, the car was there and took Mable and Jack to the funeral parlor. Mable took Jack's hand and led him in to see Jim's corpse. Jack's skin was crawling. He asked Mable how he got dressed in a suit. Mable told him that she had brought the suit over and the undertaker had put it on him.

"He's so white," Jack said.

"Yes, that's the way people look when they die," Mable said.

"Can I touch him?" Jack asked.

"You can kiss him if you want to".

Jack didn't want to kiss him, but reached in and felt of his hand and quickly pulled his hand back.

"He's so cold," Jack said.

"Yes," said Mable, and bent over the coffin and kissed Jim's forehead.

The guests started to arrive and when Mable noticed June and her husband Bill with Raymond, she asked if they would sit in the family room with her and Jack.

Shortly the organ music started. There were to be no vocals because Jim had always said that people who sang at funerals sounded like they were in pain. When the organ stopped playing, the reverend got up and read Jim's obituary and then gave a short sermon. He kept his sermon short because Mable had specified that he should. Jack was glad of the brevity of the service. But still he resented the Reverend Mathews even being at his Daddy's funeral.

As people filed past the open coffin, most women wiped their eyes. One man that Jack recognized was Claude Colling,

Claude had shared a lot and equipment barn with his dad, Claude stopped in front of the open coffin and cried openly.

"Goodbye old buddy," he cried.

At the cemetery after the coffin had been placed above the grave, the minister offered another prayer and the undertaker told Mable they should leave. As they were walking away from the grave, Jack stopped and looked back. He saw the grave diggers shoveling dirt into the grave. He broke into uncontrollable crying. He had suddenly realized that his Daddy was gone. He knew that his Daddy was dead, but even with him dead Jack felt like he was still with them. Now he knew he would never see him again. Mable was trying to comfort him while trying to control herself.

Sam saw Jack, and knew exactly what Jack was feeling. He went over and put his arm across Jack's shoulders and said, "Go ahead buddy, let it out."

Some how Jack felt the companionship and felt he was not alone, with his grief.

JACK'S BAD DAYS

After they got home, the house just felt empty to them and Jack sat down on the couch and was still crying. Mable sat down and pulled him close and they cried together. After they had cried themselves out. They went to bed but sleep was a long time coming. The first thing that popped into Jack's head the next morning was his dad lying in a cold dark grave. He tried to think of something else, but no matter, the grave thought would come back. Jack was mad, he wanted to blame someone for his dad's death. But he didn't know who to blame. He thought God was to blame, but he had been taught by Mable and his Sunday school teachers, a person should never be mad at God. Jack's personality had completely changed. He was moody all the time and never wanted to do anything. Even when he was around Raymond.

Mable was beside herself trying to cheer him up, but nothing seemed to work. She would cook his favorite meals and even bought him a new bike, but he didn't cheer up. Mable insisted on taking him to church each Sunday as she was hoping that his Sunday School teachers or someone would say something to releave his mind. Jack was quarrelsome about it, but went with her. Jack didn't like church at all. He could tolerate his Sunday school class, the rest of the service was pure torture for him. The music sounded like a herd of bellowing cows, with every old woman trying to out sing the rest. The pews were hard and it felt like his hip bones were grinding right through his butt. The part that Jack hated the most was the sermon.

The Reverend Dr. Clyde Mathews, as he liked to be called, was a fire and brimstone preacher who painted a verbal picture of God as a tyrant who was watching everyone and just waiting for them to step out of line so he could punish them. The reverend was a heavy set man, who Jack thought was fat, and as he preached he would sweat a lot. He wore his suits and his collar like they were a size too small and Jack thought he had the roundest butt he ever saw on a man. He always ended his sermons with an altar call. He sounded to Jack like he was calling everyone there a sinner and threatening them. One Sunday as he was giving the alter call he made the statement, "God will send down his lightning bolt and rid the earth of all who do not repent."

Jack took that statement to mean that was why his dad was stuck by lightning. Jack refused to go to church ever again.

Mayble was mystified by his adamant behavior but because she was a strong believer in church, she was determined to keep that approach. So she invited the reverend to dinner on Sunday. When she told Jack the preacher was coming, she could tell he didn't like the idea, and said, "Now Jack the reverend is a man of God and I expect you to be polite."

The preacher thinks he is God, Jack thought. If he said that to Mable it would make her unhappy, and he didn't want to hurt his Ma.

On Sunday, the preacher came for dinner. Mable was just finishing putting out the food and said, "Let's just sit around the table".

When they all were seated she asked the preacher to say grace. The preacher prayed, "Lord we thank you for this table you have set before us and the food you have given us and the humble hands that prepared it for us…"

My Ma set the table and my Ma bought the food at the store and her hands were not humble, Ma always washed her hands before she cooked, Jack thought. He didn't know the meaning of the word humble but he thought if the preacher said it, it was demeaning.

Mable had fixed Jack's favorite foods, fried chicken with mashed potatoes and gravy, and pickled beets. As was the norm, Mable said, "Let's all just help our selves."

The reverend grabbed the chicken platter that was sitting in front of Jack's plate and speared a drumstick, and before he passed it on to Jack, he speared the other drumstick. The drumstick was Jacks favorite piece and his dad would've always let Jack pick first. Then the reverend picked up the potatoes and took half of them for his own plate and Jack thought he was going to use all of the gravy. He reached accoss the table and forked a roll then put enough butter on it until the butter squeezed out each side. He ate like a lumber jack with his cheek swelled out like a chipmonk. He told Mable he would have to pass on the beets because they disagreed with his stomach.

He's just dumb, thought Jack.

Mable and the reverend made small talk during the meal, Jack ate in silence. All the time they were eating, Mable was hoping that Jack wouldn't notice the reverend's gluttenous table manners.

After they had their pie, of which the preacher had two pieces that amounted to half of a nine inch pie. Then the preacher said,

"Jack, let's go have a talk."

Jack didn't like the idea, but he went in and sat on the couch. The preacher came in and took a chair across from Jack, closed his eyes and prayed.

"Lord send down your redeeming grace and let thy love fill this room with your forgiving redemptive power." Then he opened his eyes, looked at Jack without smiling and said.

"I know your father's death is causing you a lot of grief, but you should rejoice, because now your father is in heaven, dressed in a robe of white and lying in the clouds of glory all day."

Jack hated to look at the preacher as the preacher talked loudly and gave Jack the feeling that the preacher was scolding him. Jack looked at the preacher defiantly and thought.

My Dad wouldn't wear a robe he would wear overalls and dress like a man and he isn't lazy, he wouldn't lay around all day and I'll never be happy because he got killed.

Then the preacher closed his eyes again and prayed, "Lord rekindle this youth's spirit and forgive his sins and let him find peace for his troubled soul."

"Now, do you feel better?" he asked Jack.

Jack said he did, but only because he knew the preacher wouldn't leave if he said no. When the preacher left Mable remarked, "Dr. Mathews always wants to help."

He sure didn't help with the dishes, Jack thought and his resentment of the reverend was stronger than it was before his visit.

Jack's attitude did not change, he still kept having thoughts of his dad in that grave.

NOT AS BAD AS IT SEEMED

Mable had other problems too. Jim had left several thousand dollars in their bank account, and an insurance policy that he had thought was substantial. Mable looked at the bank statement and figured she had enough money to last probably a year. She thought she shouldn't use the insurance money before she had to. Trying to think of ways that she could survive was overwhelming. They had their home without a loan on it and she knew nothing was pressing right soon but her mind was running from one scenario to another.

Claude Colling called and ask if he could come over. Mable hoped it wasn't more bad news. When Claude got there he told Mable that he was sorry to make her decide things so soon after Jim's passing, but he had found out that there was a date of completion clause in the contract to build a house that Jim was just about to finish.

"If that date runs out, it will cost you money, for every day beyond the completion date. Now with your permission I can finish the house on time and you can collect Jim's fee at closing."

"That will be fine, but keep track of how much I will owe you".

"Pshaw! If the rolls were reversed, who would be the first in line to do it for me? Please don't deny me the honor," Claude said. Then he told Mable, "As you know, Jim and I have a survivors deed on the lot, but Jim had a lot of equipment that he personally owned. If you like, I will take inventory of it and offer you what I think is fair price for it." Jim took good care of his stuff and I would hate to see it go to waste."

Mable trusted Claude, and was pleased to accept. Claude had been a friend as well as a business partner. He and his wife went to the same church as Jim and Mable attended and the four of them were as close as family. After Claude left, Mable was somewhat relieved, but thought it would only put off the end results for possibly a year.

A few days later the reverend Mathews knocked on Mable's door. He said he just thought he would drop by to see how she was doing. But it didn't take him long to get to what was really on his mind.

"In going through some church records today I noticed that you made a pledge of a hundred dollars to the church building fund and I normally receive ten dollars for preaching a funeral. We may have some expenses coming up and I thought you might want to give me your check."

"Yes, Jim and I made that pledge before he died. Now I don't know if I can afford it."

The preacher started reciting a long list of scriptures about how important it is to tithe and what a sin it was to renege on a pledge, and how blessed she would be for giving him the check. The truth of the matter was that he was sounding like he was preaching a sermon. Finally Mable gave him a check for one hundred dollars.

"And my officiating fee?" the preacher asked.

"Take it out of the pledge," Mable said in an irritated voice that left no doubt in the reverends mind that she felt as though she had been flim-flammed. He also knew he wasn't going to get any more money.

It only took the preacher a spit second to get out the door. A moment later another knock on her door. It was banker John, as most people called him, but few to his face.

"What do you want John?" Mable asked.

"Whoa! Did I catch you at a bad time?" John asked.

"I'm sorry I guess that did sound rude. The reverend was just here wanting money, and I guess I am a little upset".

"Yeah, I saw him leaving. He was going so fast I thought you must be shooting at him. I'm here because I think you have time to get your head together and be thinking straight. Have you applied for your Social Security yet?" he asked.

"I don't want charity," Mable said.

"It's not charity. If you'll remember, each year when you paid your taxes, the Social Security was there wanting their share of the pie. It's just like insurance, forced insurance to be sure, but insurance all the same. You shouldn't have any trouble collecting it because Jack is a minor. Did Jim have other insurance?"

"Yes, when he bought the policy, we thought two years income would be enough. But now I wish we had gotten more. I haven't applied for it yet".

"May I see the policy?" John asked.

Mable looked in a file drawer and handed the policy to John. John looked at the policy and said.

"When you call the company, to cash it, have them meet you at the bank." Then John went on, "Do you have any unpaid charges that haven't been paid? And you may have some trouble collecting."

"Yes, quite a few, but some of them are quite old."

"Bring all you have with you when you come in.I earn my money collecting delinquent bills for people among other things and I charge a fee, but I usually have pretty good results. We've been friends for so long I want to help anyway I can. I'm sure you're going to get along fine."

Then John left, and Mable felt much better, she felt that John was a whole lot better friend than the reverend was. She thought it would really help if he could collect some over-due bills.

IT DOES MEAN JACK

On Monday, Mable called John.

"Hi Mable. You doing all right today?" John asked.

"Just fine, I just got back from the Social Security office. They were very nice and I was allotted more than I expected. I called the insurance company and they said they could meet me at the bank on Thursday at ten o'clock if that's all right with you."

"Ten on Thursday. Be sure to bring your bills, and something else Mable. I meant to tell you when I was there. If you get any bills from anyone bring them to me. Quite often schemers will send out phoney charges after someone dies. Us bankers have ways to determine the legality of any bill."

When Mable got to the bank, John was out in the lobby, and saw her come in. He told her to come on in to his office. He asked her if she brought the bills. She handed him a heavy folder. The folder held all the bills and all the correspondence pertaining to them.

John started looking through them, and kept saying, "Uh hum, uh hum".

"I think I can help you with some of these; I recognize some of the names," John said.

John's secretary buzzed him and said the insurance agent was there.

"Send him in," said John.

The agent came in and took a check from his brief case and handed it toward Mable.

"Paid in full," the agent said.

John reached out and took the check and looked at it.

"There's been a mistake this should be double for accidental death."

"Lightning is not accidental; just sign this release," the agent said, and he handed Mable a pen. John blocked Mable from signing, and quoted chapter and verse about a Supreme Court decision, and lightning was indeed accidental.

"I'll have to get back with the home office, and get back to you later," said the agent.

"We'll be here," John said.

"Well I'll be! What would've happened if I had of signed?"

"You'd gotten just half your money. I've dealt with that company before."

John wasted no time collecting the bills. The first one he decided to try was one from another banker in town, Maurice Fillmore. He was a man that John had little regard for. He was a State senator and it was obvious to John that the banker was using inside information to pad his own bank account. John made an appointment to see him. They met the next morning in the office of the banker.

"Come in John. What is the reason for your visit?"

"I've been contracted to collect some unpaid bills for Mable Adams. Among them is an uncollected charge for a house you had her husband build," John said.

"I think I know the one you're talking about, it was decreed by a judge to be in my favor."

"Still unpaid though, but as you know there is a grand jury in session right now and one of my accountants has been subpoenaed."

"Are you threatening me?"

"Of course not, but my accountant might inadvertently say something that could cause the IRS to start nosing into both our banks. And as you know, neither of us would hire an accountant that is dumb enough to lie to a grand jury."

Maurice Sr., the owner of the bank was visibly shaken at the mention of the IRS. As John had suspected the banker had included the contractors cost in the cost of the house and when he sold the house the costs appeared higher than they actually were. John wouldn't have any way to make that a bargaining tool but in Maurice Sr.'s mind it could.

"Let me call my department that handles payouts and see what they can do."

"There's a ten percent collection charge on it," John said.

The next stop on John's agenda was with the Reverend Clyde Mathews.

"What can I do for you?" The reverend asked.

"I have been contracted by Mable Adams to collect some unpaid bills owed to her late husband. One of the unpaid charges is to your church for building materials."

"I'm almost sure that that bill has been paid. I'll have to check with the building committee and get back with you." The reverend had used that ploy to get rid of bill collectors before.

"Just give me the names of the building committee, and I'll check. Now who is in charge of the committee?" John asked in his most threatening voice.

An intimidating feeling came over the reverend. He was not one to kowtow but John had a way to be overbearing when he wished to be and at this time he wished to be.

"Why I am but no need to bother them, I'll just give you a check," the preacher said.

"There will be a ten percent collection fee," John said.

When John noticed that the reverend was writing the check on his personal account, he remarked "Do you know that by intermingling of fiduciary funds and private funds you are breaking a state law?"

"Why is that against the law?" asked the reverend.

"It makes it too easy for embezzlement," John replied.

"Why I would never embezzle church funds."

"Of course not," John replied as he accepted the check.

One week later, John called Mable and told her the agent was at the bank with her check, and he'd send a car for her. When Mable got to the bank they went in John's office and Mable, after giving John a quizzical look, signed after John nodded. After the agent apologized about the mistake, he left.

"Wait a while Mable, I've got something else to show you," John said.

John, took out a folder and from it pulled out several checks and handed them to Mable. The top one was one for $55,900.00, from the bank that Maurice Sr. owned.

"Oh my word, I never in my wildest dream thought you'd collect that one."

"I ought to have paid you for letting me collect that one. I had fun with it."

"Jim even took this to court and won judgment and then the judge reversed the jury's decision. It almost caused us to go into bankruptcy. We thought the judge had been threatened."

"Or paid off. Funny thing though, you only have to mention that the tax people might find out about some tax evasion, and they get scared. If you'll notice, they even paid my collection fee. I think that Al Copone getting put away for income tax problems caused a lot of people to be very honest.

Look at the next one." It was one from the Reverend Mathews.

"Jim put a new roof on the church. He donated the labor but was supposed to get reimbursed for the material. The reverend kept putting Jim off, and Jim didn't want to sue the church and finally gave up."

"Yes I know that old put off trick, that's when you have to apply a little leverage but all I had to do was ask who was on the building committee and if you'll notice that check is on the reverend's personal account. I wonder how many other unpaid bills are in his account."

Mable was wondering the same thing and the thought of her pledge money and where it ended up went through her mind.

There were several more bills that John had collected. The other bills totaled several thousand dollars. Then John got serious and told Mable, "That's quite a pile of money you have. If you invest it wisely it can create quite a bit of income for you."

Mable took John's advice, and thought she and Jack could get along very well on what John projected.

SAM AND SARAH

Sam Peebles, the owner of the Auto-Repair-Salvage yard next door, was a lean, wiry and friendly man. He and his wife of forty years, "Sarah," lived in the older part of Nixonsville in an older but well kept home. The romance of their marriage had faded, but the love and affection was still strong. Sam was at the shop five, and some times six days a week. He would get up early and fix coffee and leave before Sarah got up. Sarah would sleep later. She would have tea and always have Sam's dinner ready to take to the shop between 10:30 and 11:00 o'clock each morning. She would sit with him while he ate or sometimes go visit with Mable, then take the dishes home. Always as she was leaving, she would ask Sam if there was anything he needed from the store. His answer was always no. Sam knew Sarah loved to shop, and he knew she would have anything he needed before he knew he needed it. Sam closed the shop at 5:30 each evening, and Sarah would always have their supper ready when he got home.

Sam was pulling an old car into the yard one Saturday evening and noticed Jack sitting on the front step of Mable's house.

Jack was still having trouble getting his dad off his mind and he felt he would see his dad pull into the drive. He knew it wouldn't happen but it seemed to help if he sat there and waited.

Sam got out of the wrecker and called, "Hi Jack."

"Hi Sam," Jack called back.

Sam opened the gate and started to pull through but stopped. He got out of the wrecker and yelled to Jack.

"Hey Jack, can you give me a hand here? I'm afraid the wind will blow the gate into my wrecker." Jack went over and took hold of the gate.

"That's the way," Sam said, and he laid his arm over Jack's shoulders.

"You miss your dad don't you?"

Jack nodded.

"Well dad gummit I miss him too. He would always holler hello and wave at me any time he seen me and I got to wondering why he had to die but I think I got it figgerd out. I figger God was looking around heaven one day and most of the castles were full and God thought 'I need me some more castles built for all those people that preachers keep sendin' up here.' So he thought he needed to get some more built. 'I need me a good contractor God thought and I want the best.' So naturally, he thought of Jim 'cause Jim was the best. Then God thought 'if I got Jim that will make Jack and Mable sad.' Then God thought some more, and he thought 'Mable will take good care of Jack and Jack will grow up tall and strong and I just gotta have Jim up here.'"

As silly as Sam's tale was, it gave Jack a whole new perspective and he felt his dad liked heaven. Sam got back in the wrecker and pulled through the gate and got out and said.

"Thanks a lot Jack, hop up in here and take a ride with me." He lifted Jack up, and Jack slid over to the passenger side. As they were driving to the parking hole, Jack asked Sam,

"Do you know the reverend Mathews?"

"I heered him preach onst on account of Sarah saying I oughta," said Sam.

"Well he said God struck people with lightning because of sin. My Daddy was a good man."

"Of course he was. Like I said I only heered him preach onst, but while he was up there prancing around, and calling everybody a sinner, and telling them that they was all going to burn in hell, and don't you go telling your Ma I said this, but I thought if I got me a good hot welding rod and stuck it in his butt, he'd know what brimstone felt like!"

That made Jack laugh. In his young mind he could picture the preacher jumping up and down and holding both hands over his butt. They drove back to the gate and Jack got out and started home. Sam called after Jack,

"Thanks a lot Jack, come and see me again sometime."

Mable didn't know where Jack had been. And she asked,

"Have you been riding your bike?"

"No, I just helped Sam put a car away."

Mable got supper ready and Jack ate like his old self. After he finished eating Jack said,

"That was good Ma," and he kissed her on the cheek.

Mable was so taken back by Jack's turn around she thought Sam had a magic trick.

Jack didn't know why, but he knew he liked being around Sam. Any time he saw Sam, he was apt to go over to the shop. Each day when he got off the school bus he always looked to see if Sam was up front. If he could see Sam, he would go into the shop. Sam would greet him and always seemed to be interested in anything Jack had to say and always seem to be looking at him with an affectionate look in his eye. Sam soon learned that Jack would only come over when he could see him from the street, and Sam liked Jack's company. So he usually made himself visible when it was time for the bus.

When summer vacation came Jack spent much of his time at the shop. He would stand and watch Sam work on cars but he never touched anything unless Sam would ask him to. Jack was soaking up knowledge like what tools were called and what different auto parts were called. When Sam would ask Jack for a certain tool or a certain part, Jack would know exactly which one Sam meant and would hand it to him.

Mable became concerned about Jack spending so much time at the shop. She told Jack that he shouldn't bother Sam so much, but Jack kept going over there. So Mable went to see Sam while Jack wasn't around and told Sam if Jack was getting in the way, he should send him home.

"Shoot, he ain't gettn' in my way. I like his company," Sam said.

"You seem to have a magic wand to make Jack feel good. I try to make him feel better but I don't know what to do. I ask him why he feels bad and why he won't go to church, but all I ever get out of him is, 'I don't know.' Then he just don't talk any more and usually will just go into his room."

"Mable I think you're beating yourself up. When he says he don't know, don't you think that he thinks that if he told you he would make you feel bad? I think I know why he don't want to go to church. He don't like the preacher. To tell you the truth I don't like him. I guess if I was a preacher and thought the way the preacher does, I would be the same way, but I think I would try to find out why I was so miserable to be around," Sam said.

"We're going to get a new preacher. Reverend Mathews resigned last Sunday. He said he had been inspired by God to resign, but I think he resigned because John Harding caught him with his hand in the cookie jar," Mable said.

"That don't surprise me a bit. I hope he never gets found out though, 'cause something like that can tear a church apart and cause a lot of people to loose faith."

Sam is probably right. God forgive me for even telling Sam, Mable thought.

"But Mable, there ain't nothing you or me can do that will bring Jack out of his sad times. Only God can do that. But we can keep ourselves from worrying about it. God will heal Jack sooner or later, and you can bet he will. Jest let him be a boy and he'll figger out his own answers."

While they were eating supper Mable told Jack that the ladies of the church are all going to have a pot luck dinner at the church to welcome the new minister on Sunday after the service and she would like for him to come.

"The Reverend Mathews won't be there and you will get to see some of your friends and have fun."

"No!" was Jack's ready reply. Jack had a true dislike for preachers and consequently his dislike for church functions fell into the same category. His only experience with the clergy was with the Reverend Mathews and in his mind it was that they were all the same.

The next day, Jack wondered into to the shop. He asked as always, "What are we fixing today?"

"We got to put new brakes on this car."

Jack was standing behind Sam and just watching, and he was handing Sam the proper tools even before Sam asked for them.

"Ma told me there was a new preacher going to take over the church," Jack said.

"Yeah, I heered. They're going to have a pot luck dinner for him on Sunday. I'll probably get my fill of pie," Sam said.

"You're going? I didn't think you went to church."

"I recken I will go Sunday. Sarah wants me to, and I like to make Sarah happy. This jest seems like some special day to her."

A twinge of guilt came into Jack. Something he had not felt for a long time. He thought about his Ma, and how she tried and tried to make him happy and all he had done was pout and Jack thought about what Sam said about it being a special day to Sarah and he realized it would be a special day to his Ma.

"I'll see you later," said Jack, and he went home.

When he went in, Mable looked into the front room.

"Sam run you off?" she queried.

"No, I just got to thinking I'd like to go with you Sunday if you still want me to go."

"Of course I do," and she ran over and hugged and kissed him. And Mable thought.

That Sam, he's done it again.

RETURNING TO CHURCH

When Sunday morning rolled around Jack really didn't want to go to church but he had promised and he was even going to be cheerful. He went to the kitchen and saw that Mable had been at work cooking for hours. She had fried chickens, had deviled eggs, baked two pies and probably some other stuff that Jack didn't see.

"Isn't anybody else going to bring something?" Jack asked.

"Don't want anyone going home hungry. Why don't you take this basket out and put it in the car, and I'll get a couple of jars of pickled beets to take."

"You better get three of them because I can eat two of them myself."

Mable laughed, and Jack realized that it was the first time he had heard her laugh since Jim had died.

When Jack went to his class it seemed that everyone was happy to see him and Jack felt good to be back. In Sunday school class there were two girls that wanted to sit next to jack and Jack knew that Raymond was going to tease him about it. Too soon the bell told him it was time to go to the service. It was the part that he dreaded.

After the announcements were read and an opening prayer, a young lady got up and sang "Amazing Grace." Jack thoroughly enjoyed the song much to his surprise. She sang clearly and even looked like she was enjoying it. Then the choir sang a song and it wasn't even as bad as Jack remembered their singing. After the opening prayer, the preacher came to the podium and started his sermon.

"Hello, I'm the Reverend Dr. Norman McGuire DD. I know that's my name, because that's who the letter of introduction says I am. However, I prefer to be called Norman or if you want to be more formal, Brother Norman. I've even been known to answer to "Hey You."

A few people in the congregation chuckled. Jack was surprsed at the laughter he had never heard anyone laugh in church. Normans sermon was about what a gracious God he served, and no where in his sermon did he mention anything about God punishing people. But stayed with the theme of a merciful, loving God. Jack liked it when he said in the scriptures it is written that if we ask Jesus for peace in our souls he would deliver it. When Norman gave his altar call he merely invited people to accept the lord and find his salvation. Unlike the Reverand Mathews who would claim if a person didn't come to the altar bench and ask for forgiviness for sins that Jack didn't even know what sins the preacher was talking about then that person wasn't saved and would be condemed to burn in hell. Always Dr. Mathews would seem to be trying to give people the idea that this was their last chance.

When Norman finished his sermon the he made the announcement.

"The ladies of the church have set a lovely table in the basement and would like anyone who likes, to share it with us. I'll be down to deliver grace shortly. Please don't start serving before grace as where I will be standing, I will be first in line!"

Jack was surprised that the sermon was over. He had been listening to the new preacher and understanding the message that norman delivered without yelling or using other theatrics and above all Jack thought not trying to speak in the kings English.

After the benediction, the crowd gathered in the basement and Norman came down to deliver grace.

When the serving started, Raymond yelled, "Hey You don't take it all!"

"You better start worrying!" Norman laughed back.

Most of the adults found places in the basement. Most of the young people went outside where there were some picnic tables, but most of the young people just sat on the lawn. Norman finished his meal quickly and was going from one group to another to become acquainted. When he got to Raymond and Jack's table he asked their names and shook hands with each of them.

"I'm really happy to meet all of you, and I'll try to remember your names but please don't be offended if I get your names mixed up." Norman said as there were several others at the table.

Later as the congregation was meandering and talking to each other Norman approched Jack and Raymond.

"Do you guys play sports?" He asked. They both shook there heads.

"Do you?" asked Raymond.

"I used to love boxing," Norman said.

"How many knockouts do you have?" Raymond asked.

"None. I was a boxer, not a fighter. I won several matches, but all my decisions were by points. I only kept from getting hit and landed more punches than my opponents did."

"How do you keep from being hit in a boxing match?" asked Jack.

"Come over here out of everyone's way and I'll show you." Said Norman.

They walked to the edge of the church grounds and squared off. Norman said, "Now hit me."

Jack swung at Norman and Norman ducked. He swung again and Norman ducked again.

"Let me try," said Raymond.

"Okay give it your best shot."

Raymond swung a hard right and all of sudden Norman was behind Raymond tapping him on the shoulder. Raymond wanted to try again but Norman said he had showed off enough for one day. Norman said that the local Boy's Club was going to set up a program for boys that want to learn self defense. He told them that if they were interested, he would let them know when they have it set up. Both boys said they would like to try.

To Mable's surprise and much more to Jack's, he wanted to return to going to church. He liked Norman, and he actually looked forward to church functions. Norman would find activities that would include the young persons and Jack and Raymond usually wanted to be part of the things that were going on. Norman had a way to keep the conversations pleasant but still not violate his strong desire to please God. Norman was not afraid to laugh and wanted his congregation to recognize and enjoy the blessings of God and he was very good at presenting his belief.

Jack still liked spending time at the shop. He developed an interest in cars, and how they worked. Sam liked it when Jack would ask how something worked and was always happy and patient with Jack's curiosity. Some of the times he would go with Sam to buy cars. He often wondered why people would sell cars for junk that with very little work would be good cars and he thought he would own lots of cars someday. Some of the cars only needed to be cleaned up he thought. Jack hung around Sam the rest of the summer and when school started he would still peek in on Sam when he got off the bus each day.

In September, Norman told the boys the self defense classes were going to begin in early October. The classes would be from 6:00 until 8:00 o'clock each Friday night. Norman also told them that he could pick them up and take them to class because he was going to be teaching.

"You're going to what?" was Mable's exclamation when Jack told her about the class.

"It's not fighting Ma. It's self defense. I don't want to hurt anybody."

"Well if Brother Norman thinks it's all right, I guess it's okay by me. But don't you try to show off and pick fights and you've got to remember that it's just for fun."

Norman picked them up and when they got to the Boy's Club it wasn't what they expected. The first night they just watched films on training and so forth. Most of the boys were about Jacks age with only two older boys.

On the way home Jack and Raymond were talking about how they were going to start training and what equipment they would need.

"That one big guy said he had three knockouts on his record," said Raymond.

"I wouldn't worry about boys bragging. Usually the ones that do the most bragging are the ones who have the least to brag about," said Norman.

Both boys got training gloves, and each evening after supper they were either sparing, running, or doing some other exercise. At each meeting their skills improved. Raymond started to beef up but Jack stayed slim. Jack was afraid if he couldn't gain weight, he couldn't be a boxer. Norman encouraged him saying, "Just keep training, you're doing fine as you will see. You seem to read the other boy's movements so well, I expect you will win more matches than anyone."

THE TOURNAMENT

In February, Norman's group and two other groups decided to have a mini-tournament. Each boy would have to face two other boys in three-round matches. Raymond won both of his matches but was scored upon. Jack won both his matches and was not scored upon. All was well except Norman didn't have a twelve year old boy for the boy who won his first match to fight. The boy's father who was the coach of the boy, insisted that his boy fight Jack. This way, his boy could be the winner of the tournament.

"Your boy is a year older than Jack, and ten pounds heavier." Said Norman.

"If you think you're going to win the tournament by default, and your boy is afraid to fight you're crazy." Said the boy's father.

Jack, was in the room and overheard the conversation.

"I'll box with him," Jack offered.

Norman took Jack aside.

"Listen Jack, I know you're not afraid, so don't be bullied in to something. Winning the Tournament is not worth getting you hurt."

"I watched his first fight. He signals every punch he throws. He always glances at the hand he's is going to throw, I couldn't believe he ever landed a blow. Let me fight him."

"All right but you be careful and don't be ashamed to cover up," said Norman. "Now I watched him too. He's got a bad temper and he will start trying to over power you with shoving and clenching. When he trys that just get out of his way and land a punch when he goes by."

The first round ended with Jack having four points and the other boy zero. Jack was able to dodge or parry every punch.

The second round was going the same way and the boy was getting mad. The boy started swinging wildly. But Jack would dance out of the way when the boy charged. The boy drew back with a haymaker and charged jack, just as Jack threw a punch at the boy's jaw. Jack's punch landed much harder than Jack meant it to. Because of the boy's charge it landed twice as hard, and knocked the boy on to the canvas on his back. The referee started counting. The boy's father was holding on the ropes and yelling.

"Get up! Get up!" The referee called the boy out.

Jack was sick, that was the first time that he had ever hurt anyone, and seeing the boy lying on his back with his eyes rolled back, brought back seeing his Dad when he was hit by lightning. The vision caused that horrible time to come crashing into Jack's mind.

In the car going home Raymond was jubilant. They had won the match. Jack didn't feel like being proud. When he saw the boy lying on his back with his eyes rolled back, and when he thought of his Dad, he had almost broke out crying.

"Norman I've enjoyed the classes, but I don't want to box any more," said Jack.

"I understand, I saw the look on your face when that boy went down, but it was more his fault than it was yours. As mad as he was, and coming at you like that, you could have just held out a feather and the results would have been the same. So clear your conscience."

"Maybe, but I still don't want to fight any more."

When Jack got off the bus on Monday, as usual he peeked in on Sam. When Jack went in, Sam pointed to a newspaper clipping tacked to the wall.

"Heh heh," Sam laughed.

"Laid 'em low did'ja? Boy howdy, I sure ain't going to mess with you."

Jack read the article. There had been a freelance reporter covering the tournament and the article had a paragraph in it that said all though Jack was fighting above his class, he won with a knockout, and was the tournament winner.

"Has Ma seen the clipping?"

"I don't know, she ain't seen this one." Sam said.

"I've been putting off telling her, because I told her I wasn't going to be fighting, just learning self defense," Jack said.

"Just tell her you were teaching him not to lead with his chin!" Sam chuckled and Sam still kept the clipping on the wall, and would show it to anyone that came in.

"I don't know what to tell her," Jack said.

When Jack got home, Mable was just finishing supper, and as they ate, she brought up the subject of the tournament.

"You never told me about the tournament."

"What have you heard?" Jack asked. He was afraid that someone had told her and she would be unhappy with him and he was pretty sure she had heard something or she wouldn't have brought up the subject.

"June called today and told me the whole story." Mable said but she didn't tell Jack the whole story of what she had heard. Norman had also called her on Saturday and related the circumstances surrounding the knockout. That Jacks opponent was angry and thinking more about hurting Jack than he was thinking about boxing and his charging was as much to blame for his knockout as Jack's punch was. Norman had said other things about Jack that filled Mable with pride. Mable didn't need anyone to tell her what a great boy Jack was but she sure enjoyed hearing it.

"I should have told you and I'm sorry I didn't, but I guess I was too ashamed I'm not going to box any more."

"Don't be embarrassed. I know it was an accident, and I've never been more proud of you," Mable said. "Jim would've been proud of you too."

"You don't know what flashed through my mind when that happened. I saw Daddy lying there and I just don't want to box anymore,"

Mable's eyes swelled up and she reached across the table and patted Jack's hand.

"I know the feeling son, I get the same feeling when something reminds me of Jim. As I was coming out of the market the other day I heard a loud crash of thunder and I burst out bawling.

It seems that something is always reminding me of that awful day. I have to remind myself that although God saw fit to take Jim, he still gave me more. I had twenty good years with Jim and now I still have you and I wonder why God blesses me so much."

Jack thought that sounded a whole lot like Sam's way of thinking.

A REAL JOB

When Jack was twelve years old, Sam asked him if he would do a job for him.

"I told a man that I will rebuild an engine for him to put in a boat. That's it laying over there. Will you take it apart and clean all the parts for me?"

Jack jumped at the chance. He started and each evening he would work on it for two hours. On Friday Jack had the engine completely torn down and all the parts clean and laying out in order. He told Sam and Sam looked it all over and praised Jack for his good work. Then he handed Jack a ten dollar bill. Jack was surprised, because he had thought Sam was just letting him have some fun, not working for him.

Sam had asked Mable, if she thought it would be all right if Jack worked two hours each day after school. "He helps me a lot and he would be worth getting paid for his help. I figger he would be well worth a dollar an hour. Probably more but a dollar an hour is about all I can afford."

"As long as he enjoys it," Mable said. "You can ask him and tell him what you'd expect but it'll have to be up to him."

Jack was overjoyed. He had a real job doing what he liked to do. So, it was agreed. Jack would work each evening and Sam would pay him a dollar an hour. The next day, when Jack came into the shop and and asked the usual question. "What are we doing today?"

"I'm putting that engine back together, but I need you to drive that old Chevy down and find a spot to leave it in, and while you're down there, I think there's a car with a four barrel on it that will fit this engine. If you can find it, take it off and bring it back. Take some wrenches with you."

Jack had never driven before, but had watched Sam enough that he knew how. Sam thought Jack could do it, but kept peeking out while Jack parked the car. Jack was back in a flash with the carburetter grinning from ear to ear and he asked, "Any other cars you want me to move?"

"Not right now," Sam said.

Jack loved to drive so Sam would put off moving anything he could until Jack came in of the afternoon. Moving cars around was one of the things that took up a lot of Sam's time.

Sam was from the old school of repairing dents, and he would only fix them by reading the metal, and applying pressure after heating the metal with a torch. Sam wouldn't use body putty except on body damage on cars that had plstic parts. He taught Jack how to use a torch and pretty soon Jack was good at it too. Jack had an aptitude for mechanical work and pretty soon he could do just about any job that came in, with little or no help from Sam. Some of the jobs Sam would just let Jack do by himself. When school let out for the summer, Jack worked all day, and Sam raised his pay accordingly to the work Jack was doing. Actually, Sam was getting a lot more jobs with Jack's help. Jack took a real liking to reshaping metal and cosequently he became an exceptional body man. When classes resumed in the fall, Jack went back to his two hours a day schedule.

THE SCUFFLE

Jack was a good student. His grades were mostly C's and B's. He could have made better grades but he just didn't see the reasoning for learning how to diagram a sentence, or memorizing such things as all the presidents names or when they served, or other things like that. The one class that he only made a D in was an auto mechanics class. He thought the teacher was really stupid. The teacher would sometimes call a piston a cylinder or a shock a strut or some other misnomer. He also thought body putty was just as good as really fixing a dent. Jack would correct his teacher from time to time, and won no appreciation from him at all. Jack was also asked questions by other boys about how to put things together. Jack's ability to explain things in plain English was also a thorn in his teacher's side. Jack's low grade was because the teacher thought Jack had an attitude problem.

Jack didn't do any extra curricular activities When those things were going on, Jack was at the shop. Jack had the opportunity to play varsity sports as he loved his gym classes and had the dexterity to excel when they played something like basketball in the classes. The coaches noticed Jack's abilities and tried to get him to join their squads, but Jack had the idea that if you had to play for points or glory it would take the fun out of playing and he had also noticed how angry the coaches would get when one of the players did something wrong. He also didn't care for most of the boys that did play organized sports. It seemed to him that they had a notion that they were in an elite club and had a superior social status.

Jack got along very well with most of his teachers and had a lot of friends. His best friend was Raymond Crocker. Raymond and Jack were cousins, and when their mothers brought them to school the very first day of the first grade, and kissed them goodbye in front of everyone, they had been best friends ever since. Raymond is a carefree kind of person. He is not at all bashful and always enjoys being around people.

One day when they were together, which was most of the time, they noticed two juniors shoving a freshman back and forth between them. Jack and Raymond were sophomores. The juniors were Maurice Fillmore "the Second," as he liked to be called, and Woodrow Carmichael. They both were on the football team, both of them on the second string. Maurice was on the team because of his father's position. His father was a state senator, and had been re-elected several times. So Maurice was tolerated and passed on by his teachers and his coaches. Woodrow was a hanger-oner to Maurice. They both thought they were bulls of the woods and would bully anyone they could. As Jack and Raymond passed, Raymond suggested that they leave the kid alone in not a too polite way,

"Why don't you punks leave the kid alone?"

"Aw, we're just playing catch with the little twerp, but we would just as soon play it with you," Woodrow said.

Then he gave Raymond a shove toward Maurice. Woodrow thought Raymond being younger and slightly smaller would be afraid of himself and Maurice. Raymond threw a punch and hit Woodrow square on the nose. The punch caught Woodrow off guard and he stumbled backward and took a most ungraceful preachers seat. Maurice started to hit Raymond from behind and Jack stepped in and gave Maurice a hard right to the stomach. Maurice was bending over, gasping for breath, and throwing up some of his breakfast.

"That was a sucker punch, I wasn't looking," said Woodrow while holding his nose.

"Get up off your ass, and I'll let you see the next one coming," said Raymond.

Woodrow got up, but he and Maurice didn't want any more.

"You junk yard dogs haven't heard the last of this," said Maurice, as they left.

"I'll bet we're going to have more trouble with those two," said Raymond.

"Probably, but don't tell your folks, I don't want Ma finding out about it," said Jack.

"I'm not that stupid. Besides punching that cream puff is nothing to brag about. If you hadn't punched his stupid blow hard of a friend, I could've knocked his ass off too."

"I just thought you needed some help," Jack said.

As it turned out, any time their paths crossed, Jack or Raymond was given a wide berth. Maurice did however get the nickname junk yard dogs, spread around. Both Jack and Raymond felt the name was a badge of honor. Maurice thought a junk yard dog was slanderous because of Jack's living next to and working in the salvage yard and he thought it was a real put down. Jack and Raymond thought a junk yard dog was a loyal dog and one that took care of the owners property. Jack had no guilt feelings this time. The story of the scrap spread though the school with each student adding a bit more to it, and Maurice and Woodrow got teased about it a lot. When Maurice and Woodrow went to football practice that day most boys had heard of the scuffle, and most of them had thought of something funny to say.

"Hey, Woodrow there was a couple of girls by here looking for you. They said they wanted to kick the shit out of you and Maurice. They both had their hands tied behind their backs so it would be even."

"Let me give you a hint Woodrow, if you want to whip somebody it's better to not just sit on you ass."

"Did those eggs you had for breakfast taste as good coming out as they did going in?"

"Boy you guys must be tough, your knuckles aren't skinned a bit."

"Are you taking acting lessens Maurice? I saw you practicing taking a bow."

"Can I watch you dress out Maurice? I want to see if you've got any balls."

Both Maurice and Woodrow knew they were being completely emasculated and Maurice challenged one of the smaller boys that he was sure was afraid of him in a fight.

"You little bastard, you think it's so funny I think I'll just whip your ass."

"Oh please don't throw up on me!" the boy responded and got a big laugh from the group. Maurice took a hard swing at the boy but the boy ducked back and Maurice almost went sprawling down.

"Be careful Maurice, why you almost hit some air," another boy said and another roar of laughter ensued.

The coach was watching from a vantage spot and was hesitant until Maurice took the the swing to come out because he knew he would have to side with Maurice. But he was really enjoying the comments. The jokes didn't stop until the coach came out.

Neither Maurice nor Woodrow stayed for practice that day. Maurice had thought he was feared and admired by other students. He always let others know how important his father was, and how wealthy he was. Now Maurice realized he was only good for their disdain and their cruel jokes and he soon learned that no one was afraid of him. He also thought it was all because of Jack and he hated Jack. Actually both Maurice and Woodrow were the most unpopular players to begin with.

THE FORD

When Jack was fourteen, Sam asked him if would get the wrecker and help unload a car he had just bought. Jack got the wrecker and backed up to the trailer and couldn't believe his eyes. It was a 1940 Ford convertible. Although it was in terrible shape with one front fender dented in against a wheel and the paint so faded it was almost rust, it was love at first sight. After he parked it very carefully, as close to the shop as he could, he went in and asked Sam about it.

"What are you going to do with that Ford?"

"It's pretty old for anybody to want parts. But I figger it'll weigh out so we can make a buck or two off it."

"No! How much will you get?" Jack asked.

"I figger about fifty," Sam said.

"I want it, let me buy it." Jack said.

"Why Jack it would take weeks to even get it started," said Sam. "What do you want with a car like that?"

"That's the best looking car that was ever built. My Dad had one before he married Ma I've seen pictures of it." Jack wouldn't give in, no matter what Sam said.

"I can get it to run, and I won't work on it during work hours, and if I can't fix it then we can sell it for scrap."

"You better ask your mother fist," Sam said.

"I'll be right back," and Jack ran home and got Mable.

Mable came and looked, and wasn't impressed at all.

"It's so dirty and dented, and you won't be old enough to drive for two years."

"I don't want to drive it; I want to fix it," said Jack. Finally, Mable gave in and said, "Okay Jack, you may have some fun trying. Heavens knows you've helped me enough, you deserve to have some fun but I think that car is way past fixing."

Jack didn't know what help he had given her. He kept the lawn mowed, kept her car clean and serviced and was usually able to fix anything that needed fixing around the house but she wouldn't accept any money that he had tried to help her with. He had just saved or spent his money on his school lunches or clothes he liked. So he paid Sam, and then the first thing he bought was a big blue tarp to cover it with. Jack still worked for Sam two hours each day and when Sam would leave he would go out and work on his Ford for another two hours. Mable would hold supper for him and when he got home, Jack would tell her what he had done on the car with such enthusiasm, that Mable knew she had made the right decision about letting him buy it but she thought the new would soon wear off his having fun working on it. Mable could not have been more wrong. Jack had other things to do but the car seemed to always be on his mind. He was totally involved with his car. Each thing he did to the ford caused him to want to do more.

"You can use the tools from the shop and here's a key to the front. Just be sure you lock up when you leave," Sam had told Jack. Sam knew Jack would take good care of his tools and would make sure everything would be put back where it belonged. So Jack could get to his car on weekends also. Jack was sure to repay Sam for any expendable materials that he used and the arrangement worked out very well.

Everything that Jack would take off the car it seemed that he would see two more that he would have to take off. But he had made up his mind, that this car was going to be perfect. He worked two hours each day and most of the day on some Saturdays and Sundays. He even lifted the body off so he could strip and repaint all the under carriage. While he had the body out of the way, he checked and repaired all the power train. The motor was shot so he bargained with Sam for an engine from a later model Ford. The engine that he got to replace the one he took out was in good shape but he took it apart and completely rebuilt it. He had it rebored and replced any thing that was the least bit worn.

When he set the body back on and had it all painted inside and out, the top and the upholstery presented a problem that he knew nothing about. So he asked Mable if she could do it for him.

"I could, but I just don't have time. You can do it."

"I don't know how to sew and I don't have a sewing machine," Jack complained.

"God gave you two good hands and ten good fingers and people were sewing before the sewing machine was ever invented. Now you take the old stuff apart, and get new material and you can use the old stuff for a pattern. I'll show you how to stitch. But be real careful when you take it apart, and remember how the pieces went together."

Jack had the old top apart in a day, and two weeks later he had a new top that fit like a glove. The seats and paneling gave him more trouble, but when he finished them, using the same instructions as he did the top, they looked new and original. From an add in a specialty magazine, Jack was able to order a new set of wide, white wall tires and all the rubber moldings.

The day before he was to start his junior year of high school, he asked Sam to try it out for him. Sam came out and when Jack took the cover off, Sam couldn't believe his eyes.

"Boy-O-Boy will she run?"

"I want you to try it out for me," Jack said.

They drove it around town and a little ways up the highway and back to the shop.

"I figgered you could fix her up, but you made her into a brand new car. Boy you are something. I guess I'll have to give you your money back and drive it myself," Sam teased.

GEN HARDING

When school started Jack and and a girl named Gen Harding had an English class together.

Jack noticed Gen the first day. He thought she was the prettiest girl he had ever seen. She was a tall girl, about 5 ft., 7 in. She had blonde hair that fell to her shoulders in soft curls and was combed to perfection. Her clothing was simple and very neat, her jeans were not to tight. She had on a light blue blouse that was loose, but wrinkle free. She was friendly to everyone and seemed to smile a lot, even when she wasn't smiling, her eyes still looked as if they were. If she wore makeup it didn't show. Jack thought she was pure class.

One day Jack had just gotten off the bus, he noticed Gen standing and looking at a flat tire. The problem was obvious, but Jack asked, "You got trouble?"

"I'm near tears. I begged and begged my Daddy to let me drive to school, and on the first day look!" And she pointed at the flat.

"That's no problem, do you have a spare?"

"I don't know," Gen replied.

"Let's look in the trunk and see," Jack said.

She handed Jack the keys, and he got out the spare and the jack and in hardly any time he had the spare on and ready to go.

"Oh thank you Jack," Gen said.

"You're welcome," said Jack. "But we better hurry or we'll be late for class."

Jack was surprised that she knew his name.

That afternoon, when Jack got to the shop, and asked Sam what he needed to do. Sam told him to bring in a car that a man had left to have ball joints replaced. As jack was moving the car, Gen came into the shop.

"What can I do for you young lady?" asked Sam.

"I'm Gen Harding, and I need to see Jack Adams."

"Pleased to meet you. I'm called Sam." Then he yelled into the shop, "Jack, can you come in here?"

Jack left the car and came to the front.

"Hi again. My Daddy said that I should come in and pay you for fixing my car." Gen said.

"There's no charge, I was glad I could help."

"Well thanks again, I'll see you at school," Gen said and left.

Sam had a big grin on his face.

"Got you a little sweetie?" Asked Sam.

"No I just changed a flat tire for her today," and in an effort to get the grin off Sam's face Jack said.

"She's a nice girl, but way above my class."

That did wipe the grin off Sam's face. As a matter of fact, Sam was frowning.

"Now you listen here boy, there ain't nobody in the whole wide world that's got more class than you have," Sam said. "Now you git that through your thick skull."

Sam had never been that stern with Jack before and Jack wondered why that had made Sam mad, and he wondered also how Gen knew where he worked. He thought what he had said to her must have sounded like he was flirting with her, and she probably thought he was dumb.

At supper that night, Jack told Mable about what Sam said and how it seemed to make Sam angry.

"No mystery to me; I would be angry too if some one told me you were low class, even if you told me that. So you take heed to what Sam said."

After the tire incident, any time their paths crossed, it was always, "Hi Jack." "Hi Gen."

On Jack's birthday, Jack was up at the break of day. This was the day he was going to get his driver's license. He had been waiting for what seemed like ages for this day. Now that it was here it still seemed a long way off. He showered and got dressed and went to the kitchen where Mable was fixing breakfast.

"You want your eggs hard or soft?" asked Mable.

"No time for eggs this morning. Sam's probably waiting to take me right now."

"Slow down or you'll get a speeding ticket before you get a license. The office doesn't open until nine."

"I'm going to be late getting to school today, just tell them I over slept if they call."

"I'll tell them the truth. Don't make any sense to lie about it."

At 8:45, Jack headed for the shop.

"You ready to go Sam?"

"Just as soon as you give me the keys," said Sam then he locked the shop and they got into Jack's shiny Ford and Sam drove to the license bureau. Sam didn't think it an imposition to close the shop to take Jack to get his liciense. Sam was always happy for any of Jacks accomplishments.

Jack passed the written exam with ease since he had studied the book forward and backward. The lady that was to give him the driving test noticed his nervousness and told him that she only bit one person a day, and she just had breakfast and wasn't hungry. Actually Jack had no problem at all. When they got back to the office there was a parking lot with markers. The lady told him to drive between the markers and park in the spot that was marked. Jack had no trouble parking. They drove back to the shop and Jack ran next door, to show Mable his brand new driver's license.

"You be very careful driving," Mable said, and her worrying started.

He drove his own car to school, and it felt just as good as he imagined it would. At dinner, Jack got his tray and took a table where he and Raymond usually sat. Raymond wasn't there yet. Gen came by and asked, "May I share this table with you?"

"Of course," Jack said, and noticed that Raymond had sat down at a different table.

"Happy birth day," Gen said as she sat down.

"How did you know it's my birthday?" Jack asked.

"A little birdie told me," Gen said.

"*I'll bet that bird sitting at that table over there is the one,*" Jack thought as he realized why Raymond had chosen a different table.

"Are you going to celebrate?" Gen asked.

"My mother usually bakes a cake and brings it to the shop, and Sam will probably sing "Happy Birthday" to me."

"Sounds like fun," Gen said.

They made mostly school talk while they ate, but Jack found out a few things about her. Such as she had two sisters, and her father worked at a bank, and they lived on a horse farm, and raised horses, and she was an A student.

While they were eating Jack kept thinking, "*Maybe she might go to a show with me.*" But he never got up the nerve to ask. He wished he wasn't so bashful.

When he got to the shop, sure enough here came his Ma with a cake.

"Hot dang, I knew I was going to git me a piece of one of your cakes today," Sam said.

"You poor thing, I see Sarah bringing you food every day."

"That don't count," Sam said

Mable came in and set the cake on the counter and started dishing it up. Sam was about to start singing, when a car pulled up out front. Sam put off his song and Gen came in.

"I heard there was going to be a party here today," Gen said.

"Those darn birds just can't keep their mouths shut," Jack said.

Gen laughed, and reached out and gave his arm a squeeze. Mable was puzzled, but said," Let me cut you a piece of cake."

"I'm sorry, Ma. This is Gen Harding."

And to Gen, "This my mother Mable Adams," Jack said.

"I'm pleased to meet you, Mrs. Adams," said Gen.

"Just call me Mable."

"'Mable it is then. I've met Sam. Jack and I have the same English class."

Sam and Gen joined together in the birthday song. Their singing was no where in tune but it really livened up the party and everyone had to laughed.

"What do you think of Jack's car?" Sam asked Mable.

"Why I haven't saw it since he bought it."

"It's right behind you," said Sam.

Mable turned around and looked through the door way.

"Oh my, I better go look."

They all went out to look.

"It's nice and shiny," Gen said. She didn't know the history about it. Sam was as proud of the car as Jack was.

"Ain't he the dangest mechanic you ever seen," Sam just kept saying.

"It doesn't look like the same car." Mable said. "You really made it look pretty. It looks like a car that Jim had before we got married."

"It is like the car Daddy had I know because I've seen pictures of you and Daddy standing in front of one. I'll take you for a drive after work Ma," said Jack.

"Work? Why there ain't no work today, it's a holiday. Now Jack you take these ladies for a spin." Sam said. He wanted for Mable to know just how good it ran too.

"I want to ride in the back Seat," said Gen, thus eliminating the problem of where to sit. They drove around a while and came back to the shop. Sam started in again.

"Ain't he just the mechanic though."

"I know he's good at fixing flats, but I need to go home. My folks worry about me because I don't have a license yet."

Jack walked over to her car with her and as she slid into the seat. Jack asked, "Can I call you some time?"

"You bet," was the quick answer.

Sam whispered to Mable, "I thought I was going to have to ask her out myself."

"She seems like an awfully nice girl. I wonder if she's John's daughter; she sure favors Mae. Did you help him with fixing his car?"

"That boy don't need no help fixen' things why he's a better mechanic than I am."

Sam could not have said anything that would have made Mable more proud.

On the next Monday, Jack finally found enough nerve to ask.

"Would you go see a movie with me on Saturday?"

"I would love to," was Gen's reply." But you will have to meet my Daddy."

They decided on a matinee and Jack could meet her folks before they went. Jack didn't like the part about meeting her parents but he knew it was proper. He talked to Sam about it.

"Why I'd just go in and say I'm here to court your daughter, then I'd give her a big ole kiss and grab her hand and pull her through the door."

After Sam got through laughing at his own joke, he sobered up and said, "Why Jack you know how to act. Why if I had a daughter I'd be out shaking the bushes for someone like you."

Jack was somewhat embarrassed by Sam's remarks and wished he hadn't even mentioned anything to Sam. Mable noticed his uneasiness and volunteered her advice.

"You just be polite and you'll be fine."

On Saturday Jack drove into Gen's drive. He was surprised at the size of the house and the expance of the well manicured lawn and fields. With it's white painted fences and buildings and the neatness of everything the place just exuded prosperity. Gen came out the door and met him half way to his car. She grabbed his hand an led him inside.

JOHN & MAE HARDING

"Mom, Daddy, this is Jack Adams," Gen said.

"John Harding. Please call me John," said her dad as he shook Jack's hand.

"And I'm Mae," said her mother. "I'm Missie," said her younger sister. She came over and offered her hand and Jack shook with her and smiled at her. Missie thought, *"He sure is pretty."*

"I'm very please to meet you all," said Jack.

John was not what Jack had expected. Jack had no way of knowing, but he expected a tall slender man with horn rimmed glasses and a bow tie. Instead John was a big, muscular man in faded blue jeans and a plaid Muslin shirt, with big hands that were more like a farmer's hands than a banker's. Mae was a tall nice looking lady and Jack wondered if she always dressed up around the house. He thought Missie had nice manners for someone as young as she looked.

"How's Mable doing?" asked John.

"Fine. Do you know my mother?"

"Yes, I knew your dad too He built this house and my stables. Are you going to go into carpentry too?" John asked.

"No, I work as a mechanic in an auto repair shop, next to our house."

"Well, I'll be damned! You're the boy that Sam's always is bragging about. I never thought you and Mable's boy might be the same boy. Sam was telling me the other day at the bank that you built a 40 Ford convertible from the ground up."

"He's the one," said Gen." But shouldn't we go; so we can get good seats?"

As they left John also walked out on the porch. He let out a low whistle, and said, "Sam sure wasn't lying about the car. That's some set of wheels you have there."

"Thank you," said Jack. Jack liked it anytime someone said something about his car and right at that moment Jack knew he was going to like John.

"Boy, I'm glad that's over. I was scared to death," Jack remarked as they drove off.

"We Hardings don't very often bite people," Gen laughed. "Missie might but not very often."

No I wasn't afraid of being hurt your folks seem very nice and Missie just seems like a nice pretty young lady. I guess I was just afraid I would be embarrassed.

Jack had been taken completely by surprise when he noticed the place and the size of the house and he asked Gen if her folks were rich.

No I don't think I'm rich but Daddy works really hard and makes enough to live on and that's all anyone needs. The conversation went on and Jack found out that her father not only worked at a bank but owned the bank and the horses that they raised were show horses. Gen's manner of talk about things put Jack at ease. She seemed as much interested in Jack's family as Jack was in her's. Soon Jack felt at ease with Gen and Gen felt the same with Jack.

CONSTANT COMPANIONS

There wasn't much of a crowd at the show, but they went in anyway.

"I wanted to ask you to go with me when we ate together but I lost my nerve."

"Why would it take any nerve to ask me out?" asked Gen.

"Why would the prettiest girl in school want to go out with me?"

"The prettiest girl in school? You just haven't been paying attention. Why would I not want to go out with the heart throb of the class? You ought to hear what the other girls say about you."

"There are other girls in the class?" asked Jack, pretending that he hadn't noticed.

"You never noticed some of the cute little cheer leaders?"

"What do they say?"

"I can't remember everything. Alice told me she dropped her book and you picked it up for her and you smiled at her and she said 'I almost fainted.' I guess I just out flirted the other girls," Gen laughed.

"You were the only girl that flirted with me."

"Really? See if this sounds familiar to you. 'Oh Jack I always like it when you wear that shirt you look so good in it.' 'Jack can you reach that book for me you're so tall.' 'I saw you bowl last Saturday, you're really good!'"

"That was flirting? I thought they were just making conversation and I guess I was too bashful to keep the conversation going, or too dumb to know what was going on."

Jack had never thought that he might be attractive to girls. He had no idea that he had a "John Wayne" reputation as both the knockout and his scuffle with Maurice had been known by most of the student body and he never said much. He was tall and he thought skinny. He didn't have pumped up muscles like the boys who liked to wear clothes that showed their big biceps and showed off their manly chests. Even since he started buying his own clothes, his physique was such that he thought he looked silly wearing what clothes were the normal style. Most of the girls that he had contact with did a lot of giggling and he didn't know what the jokes were. He was a little over six feet tall and he felt too tall. Even though Gen was happy to go out with him he still thought Gen was prettier than he was handsome and had better manners and was for sure a lot smarter.

Gen by the same token had her own hang-ups. Her height was one of them. She had been taller than most boys of her own age most of her life. She was taller than her older sister and had been called bean pole a time or two. Her breasts were not as full as most girls, which in her mind made her less attractive. Most of the other girls wore so much makeup that Gen thought it looked silly. And when she tried makeup she could only use barely enough that no one would notice. She had tried to wear high heels at one time, but they were awkward and she thought just added to her height, so she stuck with leather shoes with low heels. That was one of the things that Jack felt made her attractive to him, but to Gen the shoes looked like house shoes. Jack was the first boy that had ever asked her out and she thought she was just not attractive. The real reason she had never been asked out was that most boys were intimidated by her beauty and by her being the daughter of one of the weathiest men in the county.

"I told you that I out flirted them."

"I don't remember you flirting with me."

"When I crashed your birthday party and I squeezed your arm you didn't know?"

"Actually I did see the big grin on Sam's face and that gave me a clue."

It was not a really good movie, but they sat through it all and then went out for burgers and fries. It seemed that they never ran out of anything to talk about and sat at the burger joint for a long time. Jack was really enjoying being with Gen, and Gen was enjoying being with Jack. When they got back to Gen's house, Jack walked her to the door. Gen turned to face him.

"I've had a really good time," she said.

Jack thought it proper to shake hands. But when he offered his hand Gen placed her left hand on his wrist, pushed his hand back, looked up and kissed him on the lips. It took Jack by surprise but he liked it. Gen wondered if she had done the right thing, but she liked it.

"Call me," Gen said, and went in.

They weren't really dating, but they found ways to be together almost on a daily basis. They did their home work together, either at Jack's house or Gen's. Jack was regular at church services on Sunday mornings and had invited Gen. She took a liking to the church and would go with him most of the time. Raymond who usually sat with Jack would also sit with them, and usually there was some other girl sitting with them too. Occasionally Jack and Gen would double date. Raymond's dates were usually with different girls. They joined a mixed bowling league and also went to school funtions together. When they were at Jack's, Mable always insisted that Gen have supper with them. And Jack was a supper guest at Gen's house quite often. John liked to cook on a spit and always invited jack to join them. John and Jack enjoyed each others company and when they were around each other they always kept the conversations running. On Saturdays when they had chores to do, they always did them together. Gen told Jack on one Saturday she was going to clean her mare's stall. John had stable hands that cleaned the stalls but this was Gen's favorite mare and she liked her stall to be special.

"I'll come and help, I can't think of anything I would rather do than help you shovel horse manure," Jack joked.

When he got there on Saturday, Gen was just leading the mare out to let her graze. Jack watched her walking away leading the mare and got the same feeling he had when he saw her the first iime he ever saw her. While Gen was gone, Jack got on a little tractor with a front loader to move it over where they would need it. He tried the starter and it would crank but wouldn't run. He got off and noticed a ground wire to the distributor was loose. He found a pair of pliers and tightened the wire and the tractor started. When Gen saw that he had moved the tractor, she wanted to know how he made it run.

"We've had a mechanic out to fix that three times! They get it running and before they get out of sight it quits again!"

"It ought to be okay now," said Jack.

John drove in and saw Gen driving the tractor going to dump off a load of trash from the mares stall. When she pulled back into the stables he asked Gen if the mechanic had been back.

"No, Jack fixed it."

"I'll be damned!" said John. "You keep him coming around here; we may have trouble with something else."

Jack was beaming but he wondered, "*Why would any mechanic not notice such a simple problem?*"

"He's good for other things too," Gen said.

"Yea I noticed he was pretty good on a dung fork." John teased. John had an admiration of Jack he had been around him enough to know that Jack had a level head and unlike most boys of Jack's age Jack was not a person that was impressed with himself and thought he knew it all. The admiration was not one sided. Jack thought of John as he thought of Sam. A person that knew what he was doing but was always considerate of others.

It wasn't long before the "L" word started to be used often, and not long after that the hormones started to kick in. It was a new and exiting thing for both Jack and Gen.

"Have you ever had sex?" Jack asked.

"No, have you?"

"Not unless you might call a thing I did with Raymond's cousin one time sex."

"What did you do? How old were you?"

"I was in the first grade and one Sunday we were over to Aunt June's for dinner. After dinner all the kids were playing hide and seek and she told me to hide with her in a tool shed and no one would ever find us. When we got in the shed she said she wanted to play married. Then she kissed me and said for me to look at her wee-wee. She said for me to show her mine, and she wanted to touch mine. When mine got stiff, she said if I stuck it in her and peed it was how babies were made."

"So did you stick it in her?"

"No that was the end of it. I wanted to get out of there as quick as I could. But she made me promise to never tell anyone about it."

"I didn't know little boys could be could be sexually aroused," Gen said.

"I wasn't aroused."

"You were aroused, you just didn't know what it was."

"How do you know?"

"I read a lot and I've read everything I could get my hands on about it."

"Where do you find the stuff to read?"

"At the library or any good book store," Gen said.

"Do you get aroused when we're necking?"

"Of course I do, but don't think I'm going to let you stick yours in me. I think the worst thing we could do is put ourselves in the position of getting into trouble."

"I think you're absolutely right. Raymond's cousin got pregnant when she was fifteen and they told everyone that the baby was her mother's, but no one believed them."

They made a pact that no matter how hard it would be to abstain they wouldn't have sex. They found themselves close to giving in at times but their good sense prevailed.

THE DINNER

Toward the end of the school year, Gen told Jack that Mae was planning a supper for Margaret, Gen's older sister, and her boy friend, Maurice. Mae said Gen could invite Jack.

Gen had two sisters, "Margaret" and "Missie". Margaret was a year and four months older than Gen, and Missie, four years younger than Gen. All the girls had nicknames. Margaret was called Maggie, but she had taken offense because she said it sounded like an old wash woman. So they always stayed with the name of Margaret. Gen's name was Jennifer, and she was Jen, but some school teacher said it should be spelled Gen. Missie's name was Melissa. Gen and Missie liked their nicknames. Margaret wanted to appear sophisticated and always acted aloof to Jack. Missie was a brat, not mean, but she loved to aggravate her sisters. Even touching Margaret's makeup was a capital offense, and heaven forbid when she belched or passed gas and blamed it on one of her older sisters. Gen didn't let Missie's pranks bother her. She would ignore them most of the time but sometimes Gen found Missie's jokes amusing, especially when Margret got angry.

Missie liked Jack. She thought he was handsome and he would always laugh at her antics. He also called her Missie and not like Maurice who would always called her brat or squirt or some other derogatory name. Margaret thought of Jack as someone who lived on the wrong side of the tracks and would never amount to anything and just kept coming around because he liked being around the uppercrust. John and Mae had always tried to instill in their children that people were people and what they owned had nothing to do with what kind of a person they were. Margaret though had been influenced by friends like Maurice and his crowd.

Jack declined the supper invitation.

"Are you afraid you'll scare Maurice?" asked Gen.

"Have those birds been talking again?" Jack asked.

"Every bird in school," Gen laughed.

The scuffle had gotten blown completely out of reason by everyone who passed it along. By the time Gen heard it, the story was that both Maurice and Woodrow had gone away crying. Gen however could see no sign of Jack even resembling a bully. She knew he was some what shy, but he never even thought of bragging or putting someone down. Jack wished the scrap with Maurice had never happened. He didn't want to be known for being a trouble maker.

"Aw gee, do your folks know?" asked Jack.

"I don't know, they've never said anything to me about it, but I understand why you don't want to come."

"Tell Mae that I declined because the party should be for Margaret alone but tell her I appreciate the invitation."

"To tell you the truth I'd just as soon not be there," Gen replied.

"Why don't you want to be there?"

"Oh you know, we have to put on our Sunday manners and act like we're honored to have been invited to such a fine meal and pay homage to such notable guests," Gen said sarcastically. And Maurice isn't one of my favorite people, he's always bragging and he's really rude to Missie.

Mae had the supper shortly after graduation. She hired a lady to do the cooking and serving because Margaret wanted it to be special. John sat at one end of the table and Mae at the other end. Gen and Missie were on one side. Maurice and Margaret were on the other. John had on a coat with a valuore shirt but had refused to wear a tie. Gen and Missie both wore nice dresses because of Margaret's demand that no blue jeans would be worn. Margaret wore a sleeveless blouse and a long, dark skirt. Maurice had on black trousers, a white dinner jacket, a yellow shirt and a bow tie. He had a pencil mustache that he had darkend with an eyebrow pencil and he stroked it almost cotinuously with a flair. His hair was parted in the middle and he had used so much hair dressing his head looked as if he had painted his head black. John thought he looked like a clown.

Margaret had wanted to have wine before the dinner and had told Mae that Maurice was used to having it before meals. Mae asked John if it would be okay to have wine before the dinner but she knew his answer before she asked.

John had a strong aversion to alcohol. He had been around persons who felt they needed something to give them backbone enough to feel they were socially acceptable to others and not feel inferior. He had never used drink as a crutch. But he had seen many men fall victim to strong drink and ruin the remainder of their lives.

Mae rang a little bell to start the serving. Missie thought it was funny and giggled a little and Mae gave her a look and shook her head and Missie quit her giggling. The polite talk to start the conversation was about the coming summer. John said he could hardly wait for water melon season. Mae was looking forward to planting flowers. Missie said she was going to catch a big bull frog and put it under Margaret's pillow.

"Don't start, Missie," Mae said.

The lady brought in the dinner plates with the meat and vegetables.

"What's this?" John asked.

"It's Halibut. Eat it, it's good," Said Mae.

"We have it quite often at the Country Club," Maurice said.

I don't care if they eat horse turds at the country club, John thought.

"Just wondering, I thought it was some kind of fish, by the way it smelled when it was cooking" John joked.

Both Gen and Missie thought John's remark was funny. Margaret thought it was crude. Maurice didn't recognize it as a joke and just looked puzzled.

"Are you going to play football in college?" Mae asked Maurice. That gave Maurice the opening he was looking for.

"No, although the coach begged me to. He said I could play any position I chose and even offered me the quarterback position. I hated to turn down football but the quarterback position didn't sound good to me because I like to be where the playing is rough, like a tackle or a running back, but Father and I feel I should get a law degree and relieve him of some of his responsibilities. As you know, he not only owns a bank here but has interests in other banks through out the country and even some foreign countries. All that compounded with his governmental responsibilities is way too much for one man. I of course could be of a great service to him. I know my way around the financial business. We also feel that I should entertain the idea of possibly entering into public office. The people of America deserve men of integrity to lead them. I am personal friends with many very influential people, even on the federal level. I think I'd have no trouble winning any elected position for which I choose to be a candidate."

He went on and on, all the time they were eating. It seemed to Gen it was for hours. Gen stifled a yawn and Margaret noticed it. She laid her hand on Maurice's arm and looked at Gen, with anoyance then kissed Maurice on the cheek.

"How's the junk yard dog doing?" Margaret asked.

Maurice let out a guffaw, and had a big grin on his face and was chuckling. *Margaret knew how to stop her eye rolling and her damned yawning.* He thought.

Gen glared at both of them.

"I'd rather have a good junk yard dog than a lap dog like you're slobbering on." Gen said.

John had just taken a mouth full of coffee and snorted it though his nose. He grabbed his napkin to wipe his face and also hide his mirth. He thought Gen had hit the nail right on the head.

"I'm sorry Daddy," Gen said.

"That's okay, honey, but not while I have a mouth full of coffee." He glanced at Maurice and almost snorted again.

Maurice no longer had his grin. His face was beet red. Gen could not have hurt him more if she had slapped him and John's amusement added to his embarrassment. Missie got the giggles and could not stop.

"Missie, what's so funny?" asked Margaret.

"Lap dog!" Missie was able to blurt out between giggles.

"You shut up Missie!"

"You can't make me!"

"Mother make Missie be quiet!" ordered Margaret.

"Girls Now that's enough! Missie be quiet and I think we've had enough name calling" Mae ordered. Mae was always in control of her emotions and although she could see the humor in the situation and the unsubtile bragging of Maurice, she kept her composure.

Missie's Giggles slowed down to what only sounded like subdued hiccups but the results were still the same and Maurice was so mad that he couldn't even think straight. Conversation came to a halt. Margaret tried to get the talk going again.

"I think I should study the arts. I want to be gracious hostess for the many formal functions that we will probably have to attend." Her try fell flat.

"Well it seems you two have given it a lot of thought," said Mae. Mae had the ability to act in a dignified manner in any circumstance. She thought that Gen had the right idea and could see John's and Missie's amusement was justified but she could keep her coposure.

Maurice asked to be excused. He was smarting terribly because of Gen's remark and the following pleasure that John and Missie seemed to be getting from it. Trying to cover up his embarrassment he said, "I will need to get up early in the morning, as I have some very important meetings to attend."

Probably needs to sit on his Daddy's lap and suck on a pacifier, Gen thought.

As he left Margaret walked out the door with him.

"That was an ill mannered thing that your stupid sister said in there, and that brat with her damned giggling didn't help either," Maurice said. "I didn't come here to be insulted. Your Mother should've invited that junk yard dog too and we could've laughed at his low life. He doesn't have one damned thing going for him and a junk yard dog is all he will ever be. Your damned sister is getting messed up with a scum-butt."

"They're just jealous because they don't have our class and manners," Margaret said. She put her arms around Maurice's neck and pulled him down and kissed him. Missie went over and pulled back the corner of the drapes and peeked out, then announced, "She's slobbering on the lap dog again," and the giggling resumed.

"Now that's enough Missie. You go get ready for bed." Mae ordered.

Missie started up the stairs, still giggling. Gen was sorry she had ruined Margaret's supper. But she thought, *I know where that junk yard dog business came from and that bastard has no right to put down Jack. That greasy mess thinks just because he has money thinks he is above everyone else. Jack could put him to shame any time or any way he wants to.*

"And John, you wipe that silly grin off your face." Mae said.

"After you wipe yours off, hand me the towel," said John. Then they both laughed.

"What a mess," said Mae.

"Aw crap, he had it coming. He's never called Missie any thing but stupid or something and anyone that believed that bullshit that he was putting out, needs to have their head examined. I hope he's got his belly full of us and quits coming around," John said. "He wouldn't make a wart on a real mans ass."

A MECHANIC WORTH HIS PAY

When school let out for the summer, Jack started working all day. Sam was happy with the situation, because he could take in more jobs with Jack's help, and Jack more than made up for his wages. Gen missed having Jack around and she would visit the shop often. Sam liked Gen's visits, and even looked forward to seeing her. Sam was doing some bookkeeping one day when Gen came in and as usual. He was having trouble typing. He hit the wrong key and pushed the typewriter away.

"I'll get back to that later, when this typing machine cools off," he said.

"Let me help you," Gen offered and she sat down at the desk.

"Show me what you are doing." Sam showed Gen how he always did the invoices.

"See, I put my shop name at the top, then I fix columns for prices and I type what I used here." Gen started to type and in a few minutes had one finished. She showed it to Sam.

"I'll be danged; two hours work done in two minutes!" Sam said.

"Do you have more?" Gen asked.

Sam pointed to a stack of bills. He always stapled the reciepts for parts and labor charges to the work orders.

"I'll get them the first thing in the morning," Said Gen.

The next morning Gen came in carrying a stack of papers. She showed them to Sam and all he would have to do is type in the names and the charges.

"Where did you get all those forms?"

"Made one, and the rest, came from that print shop that you drive by on your way home."

"I'll be danged," said Sam.

"I'll let you in on another secret, Jack is a pretty good typist," said Gen. Afterward she usually typed up any bills she noticed anytime she came by. Sam didn't object at all.

"You know? I can work on old cars all day, and beat my knuckles to a pulp, but nothing upsets me as much as that danged typewriter."

Summer turned into fall and back in school, Jack was about as happy as he ever had been. He loved his job which provided all the money he needed and he was with Gen most of the evenings, and a big plus was his grades. With Gen's help he was now an A student.

ALL FRIENDS

At graduation time Mae planned a supper for Gen and Jack. She also wanted Mable to be there. She didn't hire a helper for supper as she had done for Margaret's supper because Gen didn't want it to be anything formal. Mae baked a ham and sweet potatoes and Mable brought fried apples, rolls, and of course, a cake. She knew fried apples was one of John's favorite dishes. Everyone felt comfortable. Missie wanted to sit next to Jack., which was alright with everyone, so Gen and Mable sat next to each other on the other side of the table.

"What did it smell like we are having for supper Daddy?" Missie asked. she was remembering John's joke at last years dinner.

"I thought it smelled like some sort of pig," John joked. Missie giggled and everyone else just smiled.

"Margaret and Maurice won't get here until tomorrow. Margaret Said they wouldn't finish their finals until today. Probably a good thing too because with Jack here, Maurice would probably mess his pants!" John laughed.

Mae frowned at John and Missie let out a little giggle. Jack then realized that they had heard of the fight. Mae was upset by the remark because she thouhgt Jack might be embarrased about the incident and she didn't know if Mable had heard of it.

"Bird," said Jack, and pointed at Gen.

"No," said Gen, and pointed at Missie.

"Oh sure, blame it on Missie; she's only good for taking raps," Jack said as he nudged Missie.

Missie's giggles started and she started to say something.

"Let it drop Missie," Mae warned. Missie stopped giggling. She knew exactly what Mae meant, and Mae's orders were the law as far as Missie was concerned.

Mable didn't know what they were talking about by the bird talk, just thought it was merely nonsense. She did however have an idea of what John meant. She had heard from a lady at church that Jack had stopped some bully from tormenting a younger child, but not that Jack had actually punched the bully. She did however know that the bully was Maurice.

"Oh Jack! There was a fly on that piece of ham you just put in your mouth," Missie teased.

"You know, I did think it tasted funny. Why didn't you tell me Missie? Now I'll probably come down with the fly germ decease and start buzzing all the time!" Jack grinned at her.

"No you'll only get maggots in you stomach and get fat!" Missie giggled.

"But I don't want to get fat, Missie, and now it's all your fault. Aren't you ashamed?"

"You two are going to make every one sick," Gen said.

"Missie started it," Jack said.

"Did not, you ate the fly, I think you're just trying to get me in trouble and I think Mable ought to spank you." Missie kept giggling.

The banter between Missie and Jack went on through out the meal and had everyone amused even Mae and Mable had to laugh at times. After the dinner was finished they relaxed in the living room. Missie crowded in between Jack and Gen on the couch. Mable helped Mae with the dishes and then they joined the others. The conversation never ceased. It seemed that everything that came up, someone had something to add to it. After Mable and Jack left, Mae said, "Well that was better than the last graduation dinner."

"It was fine, We even had a floor show with Jack's and Missie's stand up comic routine. Jack don't say much, he's a whole lot like Mable. He don't even think he has anything to brag about. Not like Maurice did, and if you ask me he has a lot to be proud of. You'd think Mable would have a bunch of suitors; she's still attractive, and pleasant to be around," John commented.

"Well John, I suppose she's like I would be, once you've had the best of all worlds, you just wouldn't want to try anything else but now I'd better keep an eye on you. Mae teased.

THE HOME COMING

Gen was anxious for Margaret to get home. She wanted to know all about college life, and just wanted to see her big sister again. At ten o'clock she saw them drive in. They got out of the car, and Maurice got Margaret's bags out of the trunk, sat them down by the drive then got back into the car and drove off.

"That lazy bastard could have at least helped her in with her bags," Gen thought.

She went out to help with the bags and noticed that Margaret and Maurice, hadn't waited. Her enlarged midsection was very evident. She also realized what the reason for Maurice's hurry to leave was.

"How did you let this happen?" Gen asked as she pointed to the bulge.

"Don't tell me that you and…," she started to say junk dog, but quickly changed it to, "Jack haven't tried it?"

"That's none of your business. But Jack and I both have better sense than to get in your predicament."

"Do you think the folks will know?"

"Not if you can convince them that's just where you keep your spare pillow," Gen said.

As they were going in, Mae came running from the kitchen and grabbed Margaret and hugged her.

"Oh it's good to see you, let me look." She held her back and suddenly remembered.

"I've got something on the stove." And Mae returned to the kitchen.

"Do you think she noticed?"

Gen just rolled her eyes. Gen and Margaret sat down in the living room and Margaret started telling her about school.

"I'm making B's and A's, but Maurice is taking different courses and is having some difficulty."

"*Probably having trouble staying inside the lines in coloring book,*" Gen thought. *"And probably having trouble convincing everyone that he's a big shot."*

Actually Maurice had trouble finding someone to do his work for him. Maurice did think that his grades would improve in the future as he was getting better at cheating and his father had made a large contribution to the department.

"When you start college be careful, just about every boy there will hit on you, and so will a lot of the girls. I had Maurice there and didn't have any trouble. It seems to be the general consensus is that when a girl gets away from home, the first thing she wants is sex."

"I see what you mean," Gen said and pointed to Margaret's bulge.

"That was a low blow. Maurice and I are in love."

"Jack and I are in love too but we use some common sense."

"Jack won't be there, so just be careful."

"No, Jack won't be there but I have every intention of being loyal to him."

John came in and didn't mince any words.

"Whoa! When am I going to be a grand daddy?" John exclaimed.

Margaret broke into tears. Mae came running from the kitchen, where she had actually been hiding. She grabbed Margaret and hugged her close.

Gen left and as she walked out she told Missie to come with her and they would go down to the track and watch the trainers pacing the horses. Missie went along although she wanted to stay and see what John was going to do. She liked to be around the horses but she knew that Gen was getting her out of the way so the grown ups could talk.

"What do you think Daddy will do to Margaret?" Missie asked.

"I don't know but let's just stay away from them because if we're in there Margaret will be embarrassed." Gen answerd.

I'll bet Daddy will sure be mad at Maurice, don't you?" Missie asked. Gen only shrugged.

"Who's the father? Maurice?" John asked.

Margaret nodded.

"Is he going to own up to it or have his old man try to get him out of it?" John asked and he thought *The last thing in the world I want is for that bastard to become part of this family.*

"He knows Daddy, we think if we get married quietly, we can tell people we were married at school."

The phone rang and it was Maurice Sr. He had a judge from another county and said the judge could marry them. John told Margaret of the deal and he wanted to know if that was the way she wanted it.

"Yes," Margaret nodded her head.

"And to be married to Maurice?" John asked in a tone like he couldn't believe she would be so foolish. She nodded again.

"Okay, come on over," John said into the phone.

Maurice Sr., the judge, and Maurice, were there in minutes. The judge read the vows from a card. Then he pronounced them man and wife and went and stood by the door like a dog that was wanting to be let out.

Mae kissed Margaret and shook Maurice's hand, as did John. Then Maurice Sr. offered his hand to John. John shook his hand and felt that he needed to wash his hands. John's opinion of Maurice Sr. was from what he had observed and heard, that

Maurice Sr. was an unscrupulous, person who would steal the pennies off a dead man's eyes.

"I need to take care of some things, but I'll be right back," Maurice said.

John thanked the judge and wondered if he was one of the judges that Maurice Sr. had in his back pocket.

The three left, and almost immediately Margaret grabbed her stomach and all but fell on the couch. She was hemorrhaging. Mae called for an ambulance. While waiting for the ambulance she called Maurice Sr.'s house and talked to Maurice and told him they were taking Margaret to the hospital. He said that he would be right over. Mae went out and yelled to Gen that they were leaving and for them to just stay at the house.

At the hospital they found out that Margaret had miscarried. The attending doctor said stress probably caused it, but if she had had prenatal care it might not have happened.

Mae and John wanted to stay at the hospital until they felt like Margaret was out of danger. After a long wait they were alowed a visit Maurice got there about three hours later. When John told him what had happened Maurice did the most despicable thing he could do. With a big grin on his face he said so loudly that people turned to look.

"Boy, I sure dodged the bullet this time!" Then he laughed like a drunken sailor.

Both John and Mae were absolutely disgusted by him, but let it drop.

"Well, tell Margaret I'll check on her later," Maurice said and left.

"I can't believe anyone could be that insensitive or ill mannered," Mae said.

"The worthless son-of-a-bitch gets it from his old man," John replied.

A few days later, Margaret went to stay at Mae's house.

Jack thought he should that he should show his sympathy to Margaret and also to Mae. So he bought a vase of roses mingled with other flowers and took them to Margaret. Mrgaret accepted the flowers graciously although she had a small feeling of guilt. Mae however made quite a big thing of showing her thanks.

Maurice, visited one or two days usually once a week. His visits lasted less than an hour. Maurice felt uncomfortable when he visited them. Mae was courteous to him but there was a coolness that couldn't be missed. Maurice timed his visits when he was sure John wouldn't be there. With Mae's tender care, Margaret recuperated both mentally and physically and decided to go back to school. Mae of course wanted to have a going away to school party. With John's insistance it turned out to be a barbeque and water mellon feast. This time Mae did invite Jack and absolutely insisted that he come. John had it set up in the yard wih a horse-shoe court and a badminton net. John challenged everyone to a game of horse-shoes. Jack redily accepted and with some prompting Maurice accepted. Jack had no doubt that John was better than he was but he was going to give it his best shot. Jack went first and had a ringer only to see John cap it. Then Maurice tried and his horse-shoe got about half way to the pen and went rolling off into the grass. His second toss did the same.

"I'm going to have to quit this my old football injury is acting up on me." Maurice said hoping his excuse was fooling everyone.

"Probably for the best. No sense getting hurt." John said as he winked at Jack on the sly.

Maurice said he needed to get some oniment from his car and came back feeling much better. Afterward he made several trips to the bathroom and kept feeling better all the time and pretty soon everyone knew why he was feeling so much better but nobody said anything. All in all it turned into a pretty nice party. Then John started his cook-out and after they had eaten the talk turned into school planing. Jack felt pretty well left out of the school talk but listened to the chatter of what the rest of them seemed to be looking forward to. Gen was anxious about what her dorm room would be and what it would be to live on her own.

"You don't need to worry. You'll have your big sister just a phone call away. Maurice has rented an apartment and we'll live off campus."

When the day came, John and Mae watched them drive off, looking about as happy as they would if they were leaving for a funeral. Both John and Mae felt as though they were throwing Margaret to the wolves but could do nothing about it.

"I should have put a boot jack under that bastard the first day he came around," John said.

"We all have our regrets, John, I just hope that Margaret isn't compounding hers," Mae said.

"I hope she isn't too" John said. "But I can't see anything good about that bastard."

PARTING FOR A WHILE

Gen was going to start collage. But Jack was happy with his station in life. He hoped to some day own his own body shop, but for the time being to be satisfied with working for Sam. Working full time, he was making what he considered a good wage of over $365.00 per week and his savings were adding up.

On the last day before she left for school, Gen wanted Jack to drive to Culverstone and look around, and find where she would be staying. In the afternoon they drove up; it was a little over a two hours drive. There is a state college closer but Mae wanted the girls to attend the school she went to. After they found the dorm, it was getting close to supper time. Gen said a good place to eat was at a hotel resturant that she knew of.

"That's fine by me," said Jack and they had a leisurely supper.

"Now what?" Jack asked.

"Come with me," Gen answered.

She went to the desk and told the clerk she had a reservation for a double room.

"I thought we could have some privacy on our last evening together for a while." Gen said.

"Think it may be a little too private?" Jack asked.

"I think it will be just right."

Gen loved Jack so much that she thought she and Jack should be as close as Maurice and Margaret had been. She thought that Margaret's pregnancy proved complete devotion to Maurice. She didn't want it to be scandalous, but thought with privacy it would be wonderful. She thought that Margarets love for Maurice was repulsive and she couldn't stand the thought of anyone making love with him. At the same time she knew of Margaret's repulsion for Jack.

But Jack is so much more of what a man should be. He's honest and kind and sweet and never greasy looking like Maurice. Jack is so patient and I know it must be pure anguish for him that I won't give him my complete love, But I can and I'm going to do it. Gen thought.

"Are you sure?" asked Jack.

"I'm sure," Gen said.

When they got to the room The kissing and necking began and their pact was soon broken.

They sat on the side of the bed and were kissing and holding each other.

"That was certainly worth waiting for," said Jack.

They were soon writhing in ecstasy again.

"We better shower and get back," Gen said.

"Let's shower together," Jack suggested. "I hope you're not pregnant,"

"Don't worry. I've been on the pill ever since we started getting aroused in the first place. And after Margaret's problems I'm glad I was. It wasn't that I didn't trust you, but sometimes I didn't trust myself. Sometimes I would get so worked up that I would think oh what difference will one more step make and now we know. In an instant they were both relieved again.

On the way home they both started having thoughts of their soon to be separation. And the mood became solemn. Jack made the comment.

"I'm sure going to miss you during your school year. And I'm not just talking about tonight."

"I love you and I hope my set up tonight won't cause you to loose your respect for me. But I couldn't stand the thought of us parting without leaving us something to remember."

"It was a big surprise, and I certainly didn't think it would happen. It was wonderful and I feel more love for you than I ever have had," Jack said. He had some feelings for Gen that he had never known before. He felt that she belonged to him and it was a great feeling.

They drove into the drive at Gens home, and after a long lingering kiss, Gen wiped her eyes and tried to smile.

"I better not find any butt prints but mine on this seat when I get back."

"I'll put a sheet over it," Jack said.

Gen shook her fist at him, and went in.

Mae was going to take Gen to Culverstne the next day and help her set up her dorm room.

LONESOME

Jack wanted to cry, but wouldn't, He hoped Mable didn't notice his misty eyes when he got home. If Mable noticed, she didn't let on, but insisted that he have a piece of pie. Jack was having a hard time adjusting to having so much idle time on his hands. He spent a lot of his time at home with Mable. Just watching television or talking with Mable. Mable always seemed to be busy. It was apple harvesting time and she had Jack take her to an orchard where she bought six bushels of Johnathan apples.

"What are you going to do with so many apples?" asked Jack.

"Why we're going to eat them," Mable replied. Actually Mable knew she was buying more than they would eat but her canning and preserving was one of her favorite passtimes. Not all the apples would be canned as apples for pies, some would be made into jellies some would be cider some would be apple butter but none of them would go to waste.

The next week, Mable was busy peeling and canning apples. Jack could remember that all his life during summer and fall Mable seemed to be preserving what was in season at the time. She had a room in the basement that was always full of shelves loaded with canned fruits, jellies, vegetables and anything elase she could preserve. Mable knew her foods were put up in the most sanitary way and actually didn't trust commercially preserved foods. Also Jack remembered Mable fixing dishes for other people. She might take a pie to some body who was sick or fix some cookies for some children down the street, or anything or anyone she thought might need them or just appreciate them. Jack could remember one time when a lady Mable knew had a serious operation and Mable took complete meals to her family until the lady recouperated. She often baked special cakes such as cakes for birthdays or weddings for friends or anyone else that had heard of her cakes. Her baking had turned into another sorce of income for her.

One evening Jack and Mable were playing double solitaire and talking. Jack had just won another game and Mable sighed, "I wish Gen still came around, she would let me win some times."

"Maybe she just wasn't as good at it as I am," Jack said.

"Pshaw! When you two were out gallivanting around and she wanted to come by here, do you think she just wanted to eat some of my meager meals or play a silly card game with me? No she had too much John Harding in her, she just wanted to make me feel good."

"Did John play cards with you?"

No but I've know John a long time. I worked for him when he bought a resturant that I worked at. The one that is next to the bank. He wanted me to be the chef and see if I could build up the business before he sold it. When Jim died, John just sort of took me under his wing. We are still eating because he helped me get through that terrible time and we still have the nest egg that Jim left us because of his advice and it is larger now than when it started. He even collected some money for me that was owed Jim from people who are reputed to be in the mob. He may have even been threatened. I hope not, but John is afraid of no one and John is not afraid to step on peoples toes. He has a way of telling things as they are without putting people on the defensive but still getting his point across. When we were younger John and Mae attended the church we go to."

"I don't ever remember him at church."

"No they quit attending about the time that reverend Mathews took the pastorate. Gen reminds me so much of John in her way of speech; she is just like him. By the way, do you think you and Gen will get married?"

That question took Jack by surprise.

"I've thought about it a lot, but until Gen gets done with school, I've never asked."

"Maybe you should give her a ring, you wouldn't have to get married right away but at least she'd know where you stand." Mable had never wanted to nose into Jack's feelings but she thought Jack was so much in love with Gen it would make him happy if the two were married and she was so fond of Gen she thought Gen would be the perfect daughter-in-law. So Mable got up and from a closet retrieved a small box. From the box she took her engagement ring out and handed it to Jack.

"That's your ring," said Jack." I've got money enough to buy a ring."

"Yes it's my ring and it was Jim's mother's ring before it was mine. I think it was handed down at least two generations before that. Now if you would like it, I would like for you to give it to Gen. What you can do is take it to Mr. Salzman, down on the square, and have the stone put in a new setting and bring the old setting back to me. I think Gen will cherish it as much as I have."

Jack thought *I don't know if Gen is planning on us getting married. I guess I could find out and like Ma says she will know where I stand and I want to marry her but I don't know if we could get along on my salary.*

Jack took the ring, and the next morning he told Sam that he needed to run down town for a while. He went to the jewelery store, and asked Mr. Salzman if he would do it for him. Mr. Salzman looked at it through a loupe and said, "That's quite a stone you have, young man."

"It's my mother's. It's pretty old."

"Yes I can tell by the cut."

Mr. Salzman got out a tray of settings and asked if Jack saw one he liked. Jack picked one.

"The stone will go very handsomely in it. Would you like a wedding band to match?"

Jack said he would, and Mr. Salzman told him he could pick them up the next day and if they needed sized he would do it later.

Jack told Sam about the ring and told Sam he was going to propose.

"Well that sure ruins my plans" Sam said. " I was going to ask her to marry me as soon as I could figger out a way to keep Sarah from finding out about it." Then Sam sobered up and told Jack he had hoped they would get married.

THE PROPOSAL

At supper that night, Jack was telling Mable about the rings when the phone rang. Jack picked it up.

"Hello."

"This is you know who."

"Hi Betty Lou, I'll be over to pick you up right away," Jack joked.

"That's not funny, you know who this is, and I don't think you know a Betty Lou. I just called to tell you I love you and you pull that on me."

"Oh, is this you Gen? I was just about to call you. I love you too. If you can get an early start home on the Thanksgiving Holiday, I'll be up there to pick you up, and we'll drive back together."

"I can ride down with Maurice," said Gen.

"No, I want to come and get you. I'd drive around the world for an extra five minutes alone with you."

"You sweet talker, you know that flatery will get you anything."

"Then it's set." I'll be up there by three."

On Wednesday before Thanksgiving Jack was parked in front of Gen's dorm at three o'clock.

Gen came out at three thirty.

"Let's go get something to eat or at least something to drink," Jack said. "I'm as dry as a bone" then he drove to the hotel restaurant.

"Have you got something up your sleeve?" Gen asked as they pulled in.

"As a matter of fact, I have, but wait until we park."

I might have started something that is going to get out of control, Gen thought.

Jack hoped he could remember what he had rehearsed over and over in his mind. Jack killed the engine and turned to Gen.

"Gen I love you and I know you still want to finish school, but I will be honored if you will accept this ring and promise to marry me."

Gen let out a small scream and grabbed Jack's face and started kissing him.

"Yes, Yes, Yes."

They went in and only ordered salads. Gen kept holding out her hand turned backwards to see the ring. The thought of their last time they were here came back into Gen's mind.

"Do you have a room?" She asked Jack.

"No not unless you want one," Jack said.

"No I just thought you might be expecting something," Gen said.

"As wonderful as that was, I want to just love you for yourself and not for just physical relief."

"Jack, I've never known you to be so romantic and I love you so much! I don't know if I can ever do any studying or anything else now."

"Nothing has changed." Jack said "except that you've made me happy"

On the way home, they talked about how they were going to tell their folks.

"Might as well tell Ma, first, she knows what I was up to. As a matter of fact she suggested it and that diamond is out of her ring. She said it had probably been handed down several generations and thought you would like it."

"That makes it more special than ever. I hope some day I can pass it on."

"What do you think my folks will say?"

"That's why I wanted to pick you up. So Maurice won't be there to talk them out of it. I sure hope they will be happy but I wonder if they will think I'm good enough to marry you or if I can afford a wife."

"I'm sure they will be happy and if Maurice says anything he'll find out that there are two of us who can beat him up!" I wont finish school for three years do you want to wait that long?"

"I know it seems like long time but I've been thinking that we would be married ever since I first fell in love with you and I think that was on our first date."

"Do you want to know when I decided that I was going to mary you? It was the first day of English classs and I started setting my trap."

"Since were playing the one-up-man game I think I saw you first. So there!" Jack joked.

When they got to Mable's they went in and Mable had a big smile on her face. Gen held out her hand so Mable could see the ring, and they hugged each other and did a little gig dance.

"I hoped it would come to this, I love you too Gen. You were meant to be together," said Mable. "I was as nervous about Jack asking you as he was."

Jack was nervous to the point of shaking as they drove up to Gen's house. They went in and both John and Mae were in the living room. Mae started to hug Gen and noticed the ring. She couldn't miss seeing the ring as Gen was holding it out. She let out a little scream and she and Gen were doing the lady dance. Her scream startled John he jumped and then he noticed what the scream was about.

"Damn, I thought you'd seen a mouse," said John. "I told Gen you were a keeper. Congratulations," John told Jack as he shook his hand.

"We're going to wait until I finish school," Gen told them.

"Good idea," John said.

Jack and Gen left telling her folks they were going for a drive.

"I hope she don't come back pregnant," John said.

"John why do you say such a thing?"

"Well, when I gave you a ring that was the first time I got in your pants."

"And you're not going to let me forget that are you?" Mae asked.

"No way, when I do something, I do it right," John laughed. "I wanted to make a good impression."

Gen wanted to know if Sam knew about the proposal. She wanted to go by his house and tell him. Sam and Sarah both felt of themselves as family as Gen wanted them to,

After Thanksgiving, Gen went back to school, and Jack went back to work. The school year passed quickly. Jack found another car one day when he was on a buying trip with Sam. It was an older Buick that Jack thought was more dirty than worn out. He bought it because he didn't want to put so many miles on his Ford with his almost weekly trips to see Gen. He cleaned and polished it up and got new tires and it turned out to be a pretty nice car. He could drive up on Saturday morning and home Saturday evening and have several hours with her. Their times together were usually not conjugal but some times when their passion got out of control they would give in to lust.

At last the summer break began, and it was just like old times. Gen spent almost as much time at the shop as did

Jack. Sam loved having Gen there and felt that both of them were like family. Gen developed a love for cars much like Jack. And. she would go to auctions and other buying trips with Sam and Jack. she wondered why people would sell good cars at salvage prices. At one insuranse lot she noticed a 1966 Mustang that had been rear ended. At another lot she remembered another Mustang that had front end damage. She asked Jack if they could be put together and make one good car.

"Easily enough with out much trouble." Was Jack's reply.

So she asked Sam if she would give him the money would he buy them for her. Sam obliged, then she asked Jack for an estimate to fix them together.

"Just give me an estimate like you would anyone else, I want to be accurate on my figures."

When Jack was finished with the car she appraised it and had spent only half of it's value. It turned out to be her favorite car to drive. She still liked hanging around the shop. She spent most of her time to good use by doing the paper work and some times watching the counter. Jack did the work on the Mustang in the evenings but Gen kept him company all the time he was working on it. She mentioned to Sam how they could fix the cars that needed little done to them, and then sell them at the same dealer's auction where they bought them. She knew how much they gave for the cars and she knew how much they would get for fixing them. She also knew approximately how much the cars would be worth when they were fixed up. And had the idea that a person could make a living just buying cars and then selling them at the same auction.

Summer ended all to soon and Gen wanted Jack to take her up to school as he had last year.

IT DOES MEAN JACK

"I want to relive old times," she told Jack . As it turned out they did the same things, but the thrill just wasn't there. The school year dragged on and Jack's routine became almost monotonous.

SUMMER OF 1980

Finally summer vacation started. Jack made one last trip to Culverstone and brought Gen home. They spent the weekend together, except at night and Gen didn't even go to Mae's homecoming supper. When she begged off she said she really didn't want to see Maurice, and if he was there with Jack things could get ugly. Mae understood.

"I know what you mean Honey. It seems like Maurice gets more obnoxious each time we see him. He was always rude to Missie and now he puts down everything that Margaret says or does. Sometimes I have to bite my tounge to keep from setting him straight."

"Doesn't Margaret stand up for herself?"

"No she just seems to take it in stride. Margeret even had a bruise on her face when they came over one time. She said that she opened a cabinet door into her face but I have my suspicions. Missie has learned to hold her own with him and John always could. Missie played the lap dog card on him a couple of times and now he pretty much leaves her alone."

"Good for missie" Gen said. "If he got to rough with her I'll bet Daddy would take him down."

"I worry about that sometimes." Mae responded. "John doesn't like him at all and it seems that Maurice is always trying to impress him with his bragging and it just irritates the life out of John.

On Monday Jack went to work. Late in the morning Gen came to the shop. She hugged Sam and kissed him on the cheek. Jack was about to go move some cars on the lot and ask her to ride with him. Gen climbed into the wrecker with Jack and as soon as they got out of ear shot of Sam she asked,

"What in the world is the matter with Sam? He looks like death warmed over."

"I don't know, he hardly eats and he drinks Pepto-Bismol like it's going out of style. The shop is going down hill. I'm embarrassed to take my check," Jack said.

"What does his doctor say?" asked Gen.

"He won't go to a doctor; he says 'doctors can't cure anything, they just dope you up on some pill to cover up the symptoms and keep you coming back so they can make more money. If God wants me to be sick, I'll be sick and if God wants me to die, he gets to pick the time.'"

"I think Sam has more faith than most preachers do," Said Gen.

"Why is the shop going down hill?"

"Mostly from uncollected bills," Jack said.

"Don't you send out the statements?" Gen asked.

"I wanted to but Sam always says he will take care of them. He sits in front of the typewriter a lot but I think he just needs the rest. He still works on jobs that come in but it's awful hard for him to get up and down. So I try to do most of the repairs." Jack had an idea of how bad Sam was Feeling and sometimes he could get Sam to go on home close to closing time and jack would stay to close up and sometimes finish jobs up for Sam. From time to time Jack would finish a repair job that sam had only started, Jack could tell how bad Sam was feeling even if Sam didn't complain.

When they got back to the office Gen could see why they were having a cash flow problem. There was a stack of completed work orders that had been collecting for months. She asked Sam about them, and how he handled the invoices.

"I keep the work orders in this pile, and when I get a check, I just take out the one the check was for."

"Don't you send out statements of charges?"

"No, I can't get that typewriter to work any more on the envelopes. I guess I just got out of practice."

"Do you mind if I try?" Gen asked. She wanted to stay at the shop because she liked to be around Jack and she could also be helpful.

"Not at all." Sam said.

Gen went to work on the stack, At closing time she was only half way through the pile. The next morning she started back to work. She finally finished in the middle of the afternoon. A few days later the checks started rolling in.

Jack was ecstatic about the cash flow turn around.

"What about that inventory? You're going to start having to stack the cars if you get any more."

"That's your fault. You're the one who told Sam about buying fixable cars and then selling them back at the wholesale auction," said Jack.

"Haven't you sold any of them?" Gen asked.

"We've sold oodles of them, but Sam always buys more than we sell at the same auction. Sam just don't seem rational since he's been feeling so bad. But doing minor repairs turned into the quickest way to make money and Sam just seems to be out of control. Sometimes he buys cars that we can't make money on and sometimes he forgets how many he has bought."

Gen had another idea, she asked Sam if he was going to the auction on Thursday night.

"I guess I'll haft to; Jack can't do it all himself."

"Why don't you let me go with him? I can drive too."

"Dad gummit Gen, you're already doing most of my work around here."

"I know I've sort of pushed myself in around here but I love being around my two boyfriends and I'd love to do it," Gen said.

"I ought to be paying you," Sam said.

"You are paying me, I feel welcome and I'm really having fun by feeling useful."

Gen had grown up in an affluent style and her idea of happiness was not having more money.

Gen asked Jack how many cars he could have ready by Thursday. Jack had to think.

"Well let me think. Three finished, and those two Chevys only need tune ups and washed. And if we took the Buick that I've been driving to Culverstone, we could have six."

"Fine, that'll give you some breathing room, and one more week will make it all most manageable," Gen said. Gen had seen how things worked at the shop and found it interesting. It seemed to her that it would be fun to see just what could be done and how profitable it could be.

"Sam seems to be feeling better these last few days, don't you think?" Gen asked.

"Well I don't wonder, you've made me feel better for years," Jack said.

SO LONG SAM

Things seemed to be running smoothly again. On Monday morning Jack got to the shop before Sam and opened up. He put the finishing touches on a car that was to be picked up that day and pulled it out front. Sam still hadn't shown up. It wasn't like Sam to be late. Jack called his home. Sarah, Sam's wife, answered the phone.

"Hi Sarah, is Sam still there?"

"Why no Jack, he always leaves before I get up, unless he's over slept, let me go see."

Jack could hear her walking to Sam's door, and calling.

"Sam, wake up." Then in a louder voice, "Sam, wake up."

Sarah came back to the phone. "Jack can you come over? I can't wake Sam up."

"I'll be right there."

Jack started for the door and then as an afterthought, he called for an ambulance and gave them Sam's address. He knew Sam's wishes but right then he didn't care. Then he thought again and called Sarah again and told her the ambulance was coming. Jack arrived shortly after the ambulance and the medics were taking Sam's vital signs. The medic told Sarah that he had a faint pulse, and should go to the hospital. Sarah told them to take him.

Jack helped Sarah to his car and took her to the hospital. When they got to the hospital, Jacked helped Sarah into the waiting room and said he would be back after he parked his car. He had left his car in front of the emergency room and had to move it.

When Jack got back to the waiting room, a doctor came into the room. The receptionist pointed at Sarah and the doctor came over to her, and said, "I'm sorry. Your husband had an aneurysm and there was nothing we could do."

"Oh no, Jack go see, I can't believe he's gone."

The doctor motioned Jack to follow him and led Jack though a double door into a long room that was divided by curtains. He pulled back a curtain and then lifted a sheet from Sam's face.

Sam's mouth was open as if he was gasping for breath; his white hair was askew and the eerie smell of death hanged heavy in the air. Jack nodded to the doctor. He knew Sam was gone and had a sick feeling. He went back to Sarah and told her it was so.

A lady came to Sarah, and said she was sorry, but she needed some information before they left. She seated them in a cubical and sat down at a keyboard. She ask questions such as Sam's age, date of birth, etc. Sarah answered as many as she knew, some things such as Sam's Social Security number she didn't know.

"That's okay we can get that later". The lady said. "Have you any children?"

"We were never blessed. Jack was the only son Sam had."

Her answer caused Jack to choke back tears.

"You were adopted?"

"Not legally," Jack said.

"I understand," said the lady.

After a few more questions Jack drove Sarah back home and helped her in.

"Is there anything else I can do?" Jack asked.

"I'm fine, thanks for everything." Sarah had told the girl at the hospital which undertaker to call. Sarah was in the same frame of mind that Jack was. They both were in a state of shock.

Jack didn't know what to do. He drove back to the shop. The car he had left out front was gone and he guessed that the guy had found the keys and took it. Then he thought he should close the shop. He was more or less just walking around in a daze. Gen drove up and noticing the look on Jack's face she asked what was wrong.

"Sam just died."

Jack could hold it in no longer, He broke into uncontrollable sobs. Gen embraced him and they cried together unashamed.

"I don't know what to do," Jack said. "I know he didn't want to be doctored but I called an ambulance anyway. They got him to the hospital but he died anyway. I guess he knew how he wanted it."

Gen said between sobs, "Let's go tell Mable. She'll know what to do."

When they told Mable she wanted to know if Sarah was alone.

"That poor woman should not be alone. Jack take me over there."

"I knew you would know what to do," Gen said.

"There's nothing we can do, but I know Sarah should know she isn't alone."

When Mable knocked and Sarah saw her, they wept in each others arms. Mable told Jack she was going to stay for a while and she would call him if they needed him. Mable fixed some tea and found some sweet biscuits for Sarah, then she sat and listened as Sarah talked. Most of the time Mable didn't know what Sarah was talking about and sometimes Sarah was barely audible, but Mable listened all evening and most of the night. Sarah drifted off in her chair in the wee hours of the morning as Mable did. When daylight came they woke up and Mable fixed some tea with toast and eggs and got Sarah to eat some. Later, Mable called Brother Norman. Unlike the Reverend Mathews, Norman was there to help, not dictate. Mable cleaned the kitchen, and Sarah, realizing that Mable had been with her all night, thanked her and told her she should go get some rest. Brother Norman drove Mable home. Then he returned to Sarah's to help her with the arrangements.

THE TURN AROUND

The funeral was held on Wednesday. Few people attended and Sarah wanted Mable and Jack to sit in the family room with her. Jack put, a "Closed Until Later" notice on the shop. Jack had a hard time with Sam's death. Much as he had felt when his dad died. He mostly just watched television. Mable tried to tell Jack that death was just a part of life but it didn't do any good to make him feel any better. Gen came over just about every day. He would talk with her, but his mood stayed the same. On Monday Jack was up early and mowed the lawn and came back in and flopped down in front of the television again.

Sarah called Mable on the phone.

"This is Sarah."

"How are you doing Sarah?"

"Okay I guess, but I don't know what to do with myself. I need to get rid of the shop. Do you know who I might talk to?"

"I do indeed," Mable told her about John and how he had helped her. Then Mable had a suggestion of her own.

"You know, Sarah, I could have Jack open up over there."

"Oh I don't know, I just want to get rid of it. Perhaps until it sells."

"Fine," Mable said.

MABLE TO THE RESCUE

Gen came in while Mable was still on the phone. She sat down by Jack and snuggled close and kissed him. He kissed her back then returned his attention back to the television. Mable put down the phone and told Jack that Sarah wanted for him to open the shop. It did occur to Mable that she was being misleading but she had her motive.

"Aw, I don't want to open the shop," Jack said. With her hands on her hips and a disgusted look on her face Mable told Jack.

"I know you're feeling bad about Sam, and we all are, but Sarah needs your help, so go and open up. If you don't have a dent to fix, you can make one. It's the least you can do for Sam, and you know it is only right."

Gen jumped up and said, "I know where the hammer is and I can make more dents than you can fix." She grabbed his hand and pulled.

"Jack get!" Mable sternly said.

Gen pulled him through the door. When they went into the shop there sat a car with the hood up.

"That valve job was supposed to be done a week ago. I'll bet that guy is as mad as a hornet."

"How long will it take?"

"Two maybe three hours."

"You get started, and I'll go call him. He can't sting me over the phone," Gen mused.

As soon as Jack had his head on the job, Mable's medicine started to kick in.

"He wasn't upset, he understood our dilemma," Gen told Jack.

After the valve job was finished, Jack took a wiring harness off a car for another man. Then to keep Jack's mind on the shop, Gen asked if there were any more cars in the lot that they could make ready for the sale on Thursday. Jack remembered three. He got the wrecker and pulled in an SUV. It was not a car that Jack liked, but he remembered Sam buying it and Sam did have an uncanny ability to know what a car had left in it. The SUV was extremely dirty and Gen started cleaning it out the inside.

"Whoever owned this car must have only eaten at fast food joints and saved all the wrappers and change in the floor. I've already found over two dollars worth of change and finders keepers," Gen laughed.

"They didn't want to do anything to keep it running either. All that I can find wrong with it except it being dirty is a loose battery cable."

They had three more customers, and it was time to close up. Gen tallied up, and they had taken in over two hundred dollars that day.

"How much do you get paid for a day's work?" Gen asked.

" Sixty five dollars."

Gen opened the drawer and handed Jack three twenties and a five.

"Now, do you have enough money to take your girl to supper? I'll only eat sixty dollars worth."

"As long as she has a couple of dollars for the tip. But I'll have to stop by the house and clean up first."

While Jack was showering. Gen told Mable that her remedy worked.

"Sam always could pull Jack out of the blues. I figured he could do it again," Mable said.

"Jack always loves so strongly. I think that's why I love him so much," Gen said.

"Yes, but getting him to open up about what he thinks is always so hard," Mable replied.

"Yeah, you have to keep digging."

While they were eating, Gen mentioned that a car show was going on at the fairgrounds and she wanted to go. She had noticed the advertisment earlier and had the idea to get Jack's mind off Sam, that she should try to get him to go. They went to the fairgrounds and Jack parked away from the other cars to avoid door dings. They went in and looked at all the cars. As they were leaving, Jack saw Raymond and stopped to talk.

"I'll wait for you in your car," Gen said, and she went on. When she got to it, there were several people looking the Ford over. An older man asked Gen if it was her car and if it was for sale. "I didn't notice it being in the show." He said.

"It belongs to my boyfriend and I think he would rather give up his right arm. We didn't bring it to show, we just came to see the other cars."

"You should've entered it in the show, it would've probably gotten the ribbon. Let me give you my card, and I'll write an offer on the back, just in case he ever decides to part with it." The man said.

He gave her the card and Gen looked at the offer and couldn't believe it. $35,000.00.

When Jack got to the car, Gen told him about the offer. Jack thought she must mean $3500.00 which would be a pretty good profit he thought. Gen put the card in the dash box and they forgot about it. Mable called Sarah after jack had ran the shop for a week. She thought that the profit from the shop was good enough that Sarah might want Jack to just keep running it for her.

"Yes, I'm happy with Jack's work, but I don't want the worry about things that Sam always kept track of. So I still want to get rid of it. But I'm glad you called Mable; could I impose on you to go with me to see that banker you were telling me about?"

Mable didn't know what good she could do going to see John with her, but thought if it would be a comfort to her, she would. Mable wondered why Sarah didn't know John as Sam had banked with him for so long. But the way it had always been with Sarah and Sam was that Sam earned the living and Sarah took care of the home.

"I'll be glad to. Do you want me to call him for you?"

"I'd like for you to," Sarah said.

As soon as they hung up. Mable called John. She told John of Sarah's plight. John told Mable he would send a car for them at ten o'clock the next day. The next day was Saturday but John always seemed to have the time for anyone who needed his help. John was also happy doing what he made money doing. Mable called Sarah back and told her.

On Saturday a car driven by Missie pulled up in front of Mable's house at 9:45. By the time they got to Sarah's, it was ten o'clock. When they got to the bank they were a little late. John told them it was okay.

"I can't fire Missie, She's family and she loves to drive" John kidded. "Now how can I help you ladies?"

Sarah told John she wanted to sell the shop.

"Did Sam leave a will?" John asked.

Sarah produced a hand written note that read, *"I Sam Peebles leave all my earthly possessions to my wife Sarah, and my wife to the love and grace of God. Sam Peebles."*

"Short and to the point, but it will satisfy probate," John said.

"Do you have a price in mind?"

Sarah gave John an inventory that Gen had taken for Sam. The inventory was just under $90,000.00

"The inventory is a good starting point, but you have to understand that we are selling an established business. For that

I would add another $10,000 and the shop and lot are setting on about ten acres of land and there's another five acres north of the shop. I would say the land was worth a $1,000 an acre making a total price of $115,000. My commission would be $6,900 leaving you a net of $108,100.00."

Sarah was happy with what John came up with and told him to proceed. She thought that John's appraisal was extremely high because when Sam bought it he had only given $2750.00 for the whole place and all the buildings and cars. They had bought the yard in the year of 1946, shortly after Sam was released from the army and that was the last time Sarah ever had anything to do with the shop or for that matter she didn't care anything about the shop.

John also asked Sarah about her Social Security and so forth and helped her with what she should do.

Mable had hoped for a smaller price because she had hoped Jack might buy it. But she knew Jack didn't have that much.

I'VE GOT TO HAVE THAT SHOP

When she told Jack about the price, he let out low whistle. But his mind was going crazy. He knew the value of the equiptment and tools and the approximately inventory but had not given any thought to the land value or the business value. The next day, Jack was over to see John.

"How much down would I need to buy the shop?"

"Well, Jack us bankers like to loan money, but we need to be sure of getting it back. That's why we can only loan a portion of what we think the business is worth. I think you could get a loan with a down payment of $30,000 to $35,000. I know you and you seem to have pretty level head so I would qualify you for the loan."

That took the wind out of Jack's sails. He had saved over $7,000, but that wouldn't be a drop in the bucket.

"That pretty well puts me out of the game, I only have about $7,000," Jack said.

"That's a pretty good start, Jack, but everything is negotiable. First of all Sarah might lower her price or you might find a partner with some money, or you might find someone to carry a second mortgage. You think and see what you might come up with. But don't go grabbing at straws, put a pencil to everything before you make any big decisions. Because you need to see what might be down the road." John knew what Jack was feeling. He could remember back to when he was just getting started and how overwhelming everything seemed. He had worked at the bank for several years and had bought stock in it. Then the man who owned the bank died and his son let the bank get into trouble and to keep the bank from failing John bought the bank. John ran the bank for over a year before he finally felt like he could take a wage. He lived above the bank and his food was less than good as it consisted mostly of peanut butter on bread.

Jack knew what John had told him was an honest appraisal of how things were but he also knew he just had to have the shop. He told Mable what John had said.

"That's a lot of money, but I can help. Let's ask John if I could cosign or if not, I could sell some bonds and give you the down payment." Mable knew she needed the money from her bonds to live on but she thought that Jack probably could pay her back before she was in real trouble and she was willing to take the risk.

Neither of the options of Mable's were suitable to Jack. He knew that either way it would put Mable in a bind. Jack was feeling low and he thought he would go see Gen. He called Gen and asked her if she was busy and if she might want some company.

"Never too busy to see my hunk come on over."

Jack told her about his dilemma.

"I sure wouldn't ask Sarah to lower her price. Ma offered to help me but that's unsuitable to me and I am sure not going into a partnership. I just hope someone doesn't buy it out from under me".

They were sitting on the porch. Just being close to Gen made Jack feel better. Gen knew Jack was feeling low and made the suggestion to drive down by the lake. The lake was on the back of John's property. The lake covered a little over two acres and was spring feed. On the North and the east bank stood tall pines on the south and west sides was a meadow dotted with oaks. It was a place that Jack and Gen had made good use of when they wanted to be alone. She thought maybe a little cuddling might make him feel better.

"We might go skinny dipping and see what comes up," Gen teased.

Jack couldn't get the shop out of his mind, suddenly the offer came to mind.

"Do you still have that card from the guy that wanted to buy my car?"

Gen looked in the glove box and handed Jack the card. Jack pulled over and stopped. He looked at the card, tuned it over and read the offer. It read $35,000. He couldn't believe it.

I thought the offer was probably $3,500 and if I put that with what I've got I could be half way to a down payment. But if I can sell this car for any where near this price, I'll own the shop."

"Oh Jack, you can't be thinking of selling your car. It's part of you." Gen said.

"It's a material thing I can always find a car but this is my opportunity."

The next morning Jack was on the phone to Holcum enterprises. He was taken aback when the answer was, "Culverstone Bank."

"Do you have a George Holcum there?" Jack asked. The next thing he heard was, "George Holcum, how may I help you?"

"Last Monday at a car show in Nixonsville you said you were interested in a 1940 Ford convertible, are you still interested?" Jack asked.

"I'm still interested. Are you the owner?"

"I'm sorry I should have told you who I am. I'm Jack Adams. I think you talked to my girlfriend, Gen Harding."

"Yes. Have you advertised it yet?"

"No I haven't," Jack said.

"Well I can't get down there until Saturday. If you will hold off advertising it, I'll come down." A side line of Mr. Holcum was dealing in classic cars and he knew if Jack advertised it, it would probably sell quickly.

"I won't do anything then," Jack said. And he gave Mr. Holcum his address and phone number.

Saturday morning a truck pulled up in front of Mable's house. When Jack answered the door, It was Mr. Holcum. They introduced themselves and Jack came out and uncovered the car. Mr. Holcum looked it over from top to bottom and even lifted the floor mats. He lifted the hood to look at the engine and Jack pointed out that it was a '51 motor.

"Yes I noticed, those old Ford engines didn't last very long. Who rebuilt the car? The odometer has 40,000 miles on it but the interior looks new." Mr. Holcum wondered.

"I did the restoration." Jack told him.

"You must be quite the mechanic. Well will my offer buy it?"

"Sounds good to me," Jack said. His blood pressure shot up and he could hardly contain himself.

"Do you know where we can get the paperwork done on Saturday?" Mr. Holcum asked.

"I'll call and see." Jack called John and John told him to come on over. When John answered the door, Jack got another surprise. He started to introduce them when John said,

"Well hello George, good to see you, come on in."

"It's been a while John," Mr. Holcum said.

John ushered them into his office that is just off the living room and Jack produced his title. In a little while the transaction was completed. Mr. Holcum drove Jack home and Jack helped him load the car. As soon as Mr. Holcum left, Jack raced to the shop and got the wrecker and drove back to John's. When he got in he showed John a certified check for $35,000.00.

"Is this enough for a down payment?"

"More than enough. Do you want to make an offer?"

"I want to buy it at full price I don't want to bargain with Sarah," Jack said.

"It'll take probably thirty days to get all the paper work finished. Then it will be all yours."

Jack was jubilant. John got out the contract forms for the offer and while they were filling them out Gen came into where they were, and Jack said,

"Come and take a ride with me, I want you to see what I just bought."

Jack hadn't told Gen about what he was doing because he was afraid something would go wrong. When Gen saw he was driving the wrecker, she made the remark, "Boy, you have really came down in the world, but I love you anyway."

They drove to the shop.

"Is what you bought in the shop?"

"It is the shop. Come with me I want to go tell Ma."

They went in and when Mable saw them, she wanted to know what was going on.

"It's not like me to oversleep. I guess I must have not been able to get to sleep thinking about how we could get the shop. I think I've got it figured out though. Let me get some breakfast started and I'll tell you how. Sit down and after we eat, we'll talk. What are you two grinning about?"

"I've already bought the shop, Ma."

"How did you buy it?"

"You know how stupid Sarah is, I told her that I already paid her for the down payment and she had just forgot, and she signed a receipt," Jack lied with a big grin on his face.

"You mean you cheated Sarah?" Mable shouted.

"The poor old soul won't ever figure it out," Jack laughed.

"Jack, stop it. You're getting Mable upset," Gen said.

IT DOES MEAN JACK

"Aw, Ma, you aught to know better than that. I sold my car. And I got enough for the down payment."

"What? How much did you get? You only paid fifty dollars for it."

"I know how to pick 'em. But I didn't have any idea it was worth so much."

"I'll have breakfast ready pretty soon. You two just sit here and grin," Mable said with an act of agrivation and she started to the kitchen.

At breakfast Jack wanted to tell all about what he wanted to do to the shop and how much money he hoped to make. "I could build a shed back of the barn for a paint shop, and then I could let cars set in there to dry and go ahead and not worry about dust getting into the finish."

"Gen said that lot next door would make a pretty place, if they built their house on the little knoll that's in the middle of it."

"I wonder how much they'd want for the lot?" Jack said.

"If you buy the shop you'll already own it. I don't say much, but I listen a lot. And by the way, I haven't heard much about a wedding lately. Have you set a date yet?"

"I was thinking in the middle of September. The weather should be nice and if it rains we can get a tent. I'm not going back to Culverstone. I've got all my required courses for my major and if I decide on a degree, I can finish here. If I stay here, I can keep an eye on Jack. I don't know if you've noticed but he's getting to be quite a smart alec."

"I don't know if I like you calling me a smart alec. I pull one little joke and now you've got to keep an eye on me?"

"One little joke—I was about to have a heart attack!" Mable exclaimed.

"And the middle of September will be all right with me now that you've asked so nice. I was going to get another car before we get married, but now I think I'll just take you in the wrecker."

"You see what I mean, Mable?" Gen laughed.

After he took Gen home he came back home.

"Ma, I'm sorry about not keeping you up to date on the wedding, I was so wrapped up in getting the shop, that I just didn't think. Now I guess I should start thinking and making plans."

"I don't think you have any worry about the wedding. If I know Gen and Mae they will take care of the wedding. You just show up on time with a ring and an envelope for Brother Norman."

"What's Norman going to do with an envelope?"

"Take his pay out of it, Jack. It's customary to give the preacher about one day's pay. Have Raymond give it to him after the ceremony."

WEDDING PLANING

Mable was right about Gen and Mae planning the wedding. As they were eating supper Mae brought up the subject. "Gen, when are we going to start getting ready for your wedding? So far we know an approximate date, and that you want it outside. But we need to make a guest list and pick out a gown and a lot of other things. We need some time to get the invatations mailed and make reservations for the equiptment and get your gown ordered and everything".

"I don't know what the big rush is, I could go buy a dress and be back in fifteen minutes and call the preacher, and the yard is already there," John said.

"It's not that simple Daddy. This is going to be the biggest day of my life, and everything has to be perfect. Every bride wants her wedding to be the best one."

"Now John, as sweet as you are, you need to stay out of the way and leave everything to us. Just keep your pocket book handy." Mae said.

Mae and Gen started shopping and they shopped and they shopped, and in only one week they had decided on the invitations. The only thing they didn't know was how many and who to invite. Gen wanted to keep the wedding small, with about fifty guests. Mable and Jack gave her a a list of ten. Gen had several girl friends she wanted to invite. John had no family left. Margaret however gave them a list of over 150.

"These are very influential people who can help Maurice's political career. If I am going to be bridesmaid and Maurice is going to be best man, I think I should get to invite whomever I wish."

"Jack's best man is going to be Raymond, and I have two sisters both wanting to be bridesmaids," Gen said.

John had been listening to the conversation and butted in.

"First of all we're having a wedding, not a political rally, and the only way I think would be fair to the bridesmaids is a coin toss. If it's okay with you Gen."

"Seems fair," Gen said.

"I get heads," Missie said.

"Why does Missie get heads?" Margaret spouted out.

"Okay, You get heads and you flip the coin," John said. The coin came up tails.

"Well, but in all good taste, I should be the one. I think we should at least invite Maurice's father and Woodrow. Maurice should have someone on his side."

"Once again Margaret, it's a wedding. No politics and no war," John said.

Once again the shopping resumed and finally they were down to planning the ceremony itself. Jack wanted to have Norman as the minister, which was alright with everyone, and Norman's wife who was an excellent organist would provide the music. They found a place that rented equipment and they would set up the yard with trellises, chairs, and a platform for the arch and an organ. They were down to what to have for refreshments.

"Let's have a barbecue," John suggested. "I could have Elmer cater it and Elmer sure knows what to do with a pig." But John's suggestion was quickly rejected.

"Then how about a watermelon feast?"

"You know fruit might go very well, we can have fruit cups and finger sandwiches and sparkle punch," Gen said.

"Hot Damn! I knew if I kept trying I could think of something!"

"Good boy John," Mae said as she smiled at John. "We can get the cake at that little bakery down by the bank."

"No, I want Mable to bring the cake. Her cakes make bakery cakes look like moon pies, and I've already asked her."

"Moon pies. Now there's an idea!"

"Be quiet Daddy," Gen laughed.

THE WEDDING

Jack had taken Mable's advice and let Gen and Mae take care of the wedding plans. But he had scheduled so much work, that he was working twelve hour days. Especially since he had closed on buying the shop. He wanted to have another car for himself to drive and enough time for a honeymoon. But he was managing. He had found out that running the business was a whole lot harder to do by himself and understood that Sam was smarter than he had guessed. Even things like moving cars or filling out bills ect. took time that he needed to do repairs. But he was determined that he was going to make a go of it. The hours that he worked after closing the shop each day were the most productive. He could do jobs and not be interupted by customers during the evening. The only thing was that he wasn't seeing Gen as much as he wanted to. Gen didn't like not being with Jack either. So she would come over about every day and help him with his bills and anything else she could do.

All too soon it was the day for the wedding.

Jack was up early after a mostly sleepless night. He had ran over and over in his mind about everything he'd need to have done before the wedding, and no matter how many times he assured himself, it would all start over again. He had his bag packed, his tux for himself and one for Raymond, his car was ready, and he had money and time for the honeymoon. He finally got up and showered and went to the kitchen. Mable was just finishing the cake.

"Good morning honey, did you sleep good? I'll fix breakfast in just a minute."

"I don't think I can eat. And how am I going to drive and hold the cake?"

"Everything is taken care of. Raymond is going to take the cake and then come back and get me and Sarah," Mable told him. Raymond was an unsung hero. If someone needed help or something done Raymond always seemed to be the person to call.

Gen had slept well enough, but as soon as she woke up she started worrying. The people who were to do the set up of the trellises and chairs hadn't even got there yet, and the people that were going to put the flowers on the trellises couldn't start until everything else was in place. John was still working in the stables and hadn't even started to get ready, and Mae had a dozen things to do before she got ready. Mae had the same problem as Mable, but with the bride.

"Just you simmer down, everything is going fine, if it isn't we'll take care of it. Look outside it's a beautiful day. Let's enjoy it." In fact it was a beautiful day, the trees were still green but there was a smell of fall in the air with the heat of summer mostly over.

Why didn't we just run off and get married? Gen thought.

Everything got put in place, and then Gen found other things to worry about.

"It might rain or. O God what if Jack has changed his mind?"

While Mae and Missie were helping her dress and telling her how pretty she was Gen kept looking out the window. The guests were beginning to arrive and where was Jack? She saw Norman and his wife getting under the arch and at the organ, but no Jack. When she was about to panic, there he was, and Norman was showing him where to stand.

Mae left to take her seat.

The music started and Gen and Missie went down and joined Raymond and John. Raymond with Missie on his arm walked up the makeshift isle and took their places. The wedding march started and John, with Gen on his arm, came up the isle and stopped in front of the preacher.

"Who gives this woman to be married?" Norman asked.

"Her Mother and I," John said, and he gave Jack her hand and sat down next to Mae.

After "Dearly beloved," neither Gen nor Jack heard anything Norman said until they heard, "Do you Jack, and do you Gen…." After the "I dos" were said, Norman pronounced them man and wife.

"You may kiss your bride."

After the kiss they turned and faced the guests and Norman said, "Ladies and gentlemen, may I present to you Mr. and Mrs. Jack Adams."

The audience applauded politely, and Maurice stood up and yelled,"yaw hoo!" and laughed with what John had named his idiot laugh. Raymond moved close to Jack's ear and in a low voice said, "I'd like to teach that bastard some manners." Jack nodded.

In the receiving line the men were kissing Gen on the cheek and shaking Jack's hand while the women were kissing both Gen and Jack. When Missie got to Jack, she hugged him and kissed him on his lips. Missie felt a tingle.

After the bouquet toss and the garter flip, Jack and Gen were about to cut the cake when Gen noticed a moon pie next to the cake. She picked it up and waved it in John's direction and laughed. "Daddy!"

John put on his most innocent face and held his palms forward. Mae was standing close to Mable both decked out in their finest dresses with white gloves, hats, and white shoes, and Mae told Mable, "I'm going to have to shoot John some of these days."

The reception went off with out a hitch except for Maurice going around trying to be the life of the party. He would shake anyone's hand that would shake with him and was making crude remarks to anyone who would listen. He kept going to his car and getting more drunken and in general was a big embarrassment to Mae and John. Then Maurice started to mouth off to Raymond and John thought Raymond might punch Maurice out. Raymond kept trying to ignore him but Maurice kept trying to put him and Jack down. Each time Raymond would try to walk away Maurice would follow and try saying something else to put down Jack or just the wedding in general. Margaret was walking around, with her nose so high that people thought she had a stiff neck. Finally John took Margaret aside and asked her to take Maurice home. She was offended but by this time even she could see that Maurice could barely stand up and could see that he was stepping over the line by agrivating Raymond so she did as John wished. As they drove away Maurice was sticking his head out the car window and laughing while yelling congratulations!

Soon Jack and Gen left in Jack's beautifully restored 1955, dark maroon Cadillac convertible which had a "Just Married" banner tied to the back. They started for Niagara Falls. Jack had to stop at Mable's house to leave his rented tux so that Raymond could return it. Then off to Niagara. But when they got to Culverstone they remembered the hotel and decided to spend the night.

The honeymoon was great but they spent more time looking at each other than they did looking at the falls.

On the way back, as they were driving through Culverstone, Gen noticed a building with a sign that read, "HOLCUM ENTERPRIZES."

"Jack stop!" Gen exclaimed as she noticed in the front window of the business, sat Jack's Ford.

Let's go in and look," Gen suggested.

They were looking at the Ford that had a price of $75,000 on a little card in the windshield.

George came to the front from where he was polishing on an old Buick.

"Hi Jack, do you have another car for me?" He asked as he noticed the Caddy out front. Then he turned to Gen and spoke to her.

"No, we just saw the Ford, and wanted to see it again," Jack said.

"Can't blame you, it's my favorite right now, but I don't think it's going to be here long. You really did a bangup job on restoration even the floors and under works look new."

Jack was feeling proud about his praise from Mr. Yocum, and said.

"That was my first try. I wanted everything to be perfect,"

"Well you suceeded." Mr. Yocum replied.

As they drove off, Jack asked, "Did you see the price he is asking?"

"Sure did. You may have sold it too cheap," Gen said.

THE APARTMENT

When they got back, they rented a one bedroom furnished apartment. The apartment was a nice place but it was not like either of them had been used to. It only had an outside parking space so Jack would drive one of the other cars home each night. It was no problem for Gen, she loved the simplicity of it and especially the closeness. To Gen the apartment felt like her play house when she was little. She would be in the little house that john had a man build and envision her husband and children. Jack fit the way her husband had been in her imagination. The shop was doing fine, since Gen was also staying at the shop most days and really helped out, but Jack started worrying. He had never had mortgage before and living in an apartment and buying their own food, they couldn't save very much. He also thought Gen should have more. He told Gen his thoughts. Gen wasn't worried at all. She was happy with the situation. So far as she was concerned they were comfortable and had all the money they needed and living with jack was more than she had ever expected. But to ease Jack's mind she said.

"Jack I think you are worrying needlessly. We are eating regularly and sleeping warm and so far as the savings. I don't think we have any worries. Sure we aren't adding much to our bank account but we have other resources if we should experience a slow down, we've got two very marketable cars with your Caddy and my Mustang. But if you're so worried. Then we'll just have to make more. And one more thing I want you to know, I'm enjoying every minute of every day I live with you and I won't change my mind."

"How are we going to make more? We're staying busy at the shop, and I don't see how we could do any more. I love you Gen and I'm certainly not sorry we got married. I certainly don't have any regrets and I wasn't insinuating that. But I want us to be as comfotable as you always were.

"Well," Gen said, "I'm just about as comfortable as I have ever been but let's take a look at what we're doing and find ways to do them better. The insurance jobs are coming in pretty well and I think we're bidding them too low. If we bid them just a little bit higher, we may lose some of them, but when you only make your wages on them, the shop doesn't make any profit at all. The cars we trade at the auction are the most profitable. That SUV we sold netted over $500. The mid-sized cars come in next with little body repair, mainly because we can buy them so cheap. And I know you don't like SUV's or pick-ups but they're usually cheap to buy and higher when they are lot ready. And did you know that the barn at the back of the shop is full of old motor blocks?"

"Of course that's where we keep them."

"Why keep them? I know Sam made a good living off the yard and shop, and we can too. But Sam did a lot of things that just didn't make good business sense. I think I know why he kept the blocks separated. Because pure cast is worth more than mixed scrap. But Sam just never got around to selling it. The company that hauls off our stripped cars also buys cast. I think if we called them we could get good money for the blocks right now."

"I'll look up their number and give them a call when we get back to the shop," Jack said.

"Boy I'm glad I met you. I just thought you were the best looking girl in school, but now I find out that along with all your other attributes you've got a brain that just won't quit."

"My greatest accomplishment is my ability to pick out the greatest man in the world," Gen said. We'll be all right you'll see and I think we'll have a lot of fun getting there.

"Aw you're just trying to get me in the sack." Jack teased.

"You can always see right through me," Gen giggled.

Jack called the next morning and talked to David McCurey the owner of "JOE'S SCRAP METAL." David said he would send a trailer and if they would load the blocks he would like to buy them. After almost three trailer loads, Jack received a check for $2,585. Jack found out in a hurry why Sam had not had the blocks hauled off. Even with Gen running the wrecker it was a back breaking job. They tried hooking a chain through the cylinder holes first and lifting the blocks and putting them in place. But Jack would have to climb into the trailer each time to unhook the chain. Then Jack got an idea to make a spring loaded pair of tongs so they could just hold them in place until the lifting started, and then when they were let down in the trailer the tongs would release, and they could just leave them without manually unhooking them. Even by using the tongs, it still took almost all day to load a trailer. After they got the barn completely emptied Jack was three days behind with his other work.

"Now," Jack said, "Shall we fill it up again?"

"No, let's put good parts in there and tag them all so I can keep track of what we've got."

Spending the time to get rid of the blocks, got Jack behind on his jobs again. So he started putting in twelve hours a day again. Gen also stayed and helped or sometimes she would go over and visit with Mable and help Mable with fixing supper and they would eat with Mable. Gen would go shopping with Mable and insist on paying for the groceries. Gen liked being around Mable. She was learning more about cooking than she had ever learned at home and on their shopping trips she was learnig how to be very frugal buying groceries. Both Gen and Jack would work like there was no tomorrow during the week but on Saturday they were up and running to any city within three or four hours driving time looking for cars they could make money on and staying in luxury hotels on tax deductible expenses. Gen suggested the trips because she thought it would give Jack a change of routine and keep him from worrying. Both Gen and Jack loved every trip, even though they drove there in a truck pulling a trailer. However, the new soon wore off their new found way of buying and monotony set in. Soon luxury hotels seemed to become a hassle rather than an excitement, and they longed for a slower more relaxing pace. Their inventory for salvage was at an all time low. Even Jack was loosing his enthusiasm about salvage. Gen however still was as energetic as ever. She thought the fence around the lot needed to be painted white, and she rented a sprayer and painted it. She thought the yard was too weedy and she borrowed John's bush hog and took care of the weeds. She wished she could get Jack to be happy with their apartment. Then inspiration struck. She asked Jack why they kept the part of the shop directly behind the office half full of shelves of old things such as starters and generators and alternators. "That's just where Sam always kept them," Jack said.

"Are they all good?" Gen asked.

"You know I couldn't tell you. If I take one off I just put it with the rest of them."

"But we only get five dollars for them," Gen said. "I've got an idea. If we get rid of all of them and put the shelves in the barn where we had the motor blocks, then we could partition off that half of the shop and put an apartment in it." Jack gave it some thought and liked the idea.

"But that would take all the money we got for the blocks and then some. Where's the profit in that?"

"Right now, We're flushing $500 a month down the drain for an apartment that you hate. We would save it all back in six months."

"Does David buy stuff like the starters?"

"I don't know, but I've found out that there is a factory over in the industrial park that rebuilds starters and generators and they pay over half as much for salvaged ones as we get. And that's mill run, working or not. We can sell all we have and have enough to do the apartment."

While visiting John and Mae, Gen told them of their plans for an apartment. John was enthusiastic about it but Mae couldn't visualize it. She could only imagine it as a dirty dark room. Margaret and Maurice heard about it from Mae.

"She's planning to live in a junk yard?" Margaret screamed.

"I think where a man lives says a whole lot about him," Maurice said.

John said, in no uncertain terms, "I respect Gen and Jack for doing for themselves and I think what a man does and when a man brags about what he says he's going to do sometime says a hell of a lot more about him."

Maurice reddened and had no answer. As Mae nodded in agreement.

Gen lost no time. She borrowed John's pick-up and started hauling the things to sell. After three big loads she had the room empty and another $1,565 to go toward the apartment. That evening she and Jack, using the wrecker, moved all the shelves to the barn. Jack had all he could do keeping up with the body repair jobs. Raising the price on his bids didn't seem to slow down his winning of bids and he had picked up another client, George Holcum. He saw Jack at an insurance lot one day and George had just bought a '51 Chevy. George asked Jack for a bid and accepted the bid. Jack had bid the job high, but George didn't bat an eye because he knew Jack's work and he wanted his cars first class. Gen had learned the bidding process and had taken over much of the bidding for Jack as well as watching the front desk. Actually Gen usually bid the jobs higher than Jack would have, but it worked for her. While Gen watched the front, she was also drawing plans for the apartment. She showed her plans to Jack and his enthusiasm renewed. The apartment was to be forty feet long and thirty feet wide. The entrance would be on the north with a windowed door, the bedroom on the east with a window on the north, and the bath room and utility room taking up the reminder of the east end. There was room in the middle for the living room with a large window and a back door. The kitchen and dining room took the other end. There was little need for digging as the pipes for the kitchen ran down inside the wall. With Jack's work load, and being determined to keep it in budget, they decided to build it in the evenings and on weekends. They soon had the frame built. Jack didn't trust his electrical knowledge for the wiring, so they hired an electrician. John came over on one weekend and he and Jack together cut the windows and doors and hung the wall board. Mable wanted to help too so she fixed their meals for dinner and supper each day. One week later, they had it all mudded in and painted. Gen found the cabinets at a garage sale, and the range at a second hand store. By the time they had the tile work finished and floors carpeted they were out of all the budget money they had allotted and they still didn't have it furnished.

Gen was so disappointed she didn't know what to do, and hated telling Jack. Jack on the other hand thought they had really done a great job.

"I'm sorry Jack, I really thought we could do it."

"We gave it our best shot, didn't we? If this is the biggest problem we ever have we are going to have one hell of a life together. I've been watching you breaking your back for over two months. Now we can settle down and enjoy ourselves. I do want to do one more thing on the cheap side though, I want to keep my old bedroom furniture but I think we have plenty of money to buy everything else."

"Great do you think it will be okay with Mable if we take your bed and stuff?"

Mable was delighted, because Jim had made the furniture for Jack. After they closed the shop, they moved the furniture into their new apartment. Mable brought over some clean bed clothes and helped Gen make up the bed. She and Gen Gloated over it how the room looked.

"I'm going to spend the night," Jack said.

"Not without me," Gen said.

"Come over for breakfast," Mable said, and left.

Gen was anxious to have her house warming, so she lost no time furnishing the house. They never spent another night in their first apartment. Gen was not finished yet. She had a small porch built to the north of the door and had banisters on each side with a gabled roof supported by two turned posts. She mowed a square for a front lawn and fixed a driveway from the road.

"Now people will know where we live and won't be trying to get in through the shop."

HOME SWEET HOME

With Mable's help Gen planned her inaugural supper as she called it and invited John, Mae, Missie and Mable. She didn't invite Margaret because she didn't want Maurice in her house. Maurice and Margaret had graduated by this time and Maurice was trying to get on the county ballot and run for sheriff. and he was more loud-mouthed and irritating than ever.

Mae was really surprised at how nice it turned out. By entering from the north, it seemed like going into any other house.

"This brings back some of our days, Don't it John?" Mae said. "Remember when we got married and we lived upstairs over the bank?"

"Yeah I remember, I still can't believe you married me as poverty stricken as I was. And your dad didn't think I would ever be able to feed you."

John was impressed, and said so. Mable was as happy and proud as she could be. Missie said, "It's really cool." And she thought, *"Gen has everything a girl could want—this home and is married to Jack."*

After dinner John said he needed a cigar. He and Jack went out to where Gen had mowed the grass in preparation of fencing in a front yard. John lit his cigar and said,

"Jack it looks like you and Gen have it going your way. You two seem to know what you want and are going after it. You seem, so far as I can see, to run a very profitable business. You continue to double up on your mortgage payments. And this is none of my business, but you seem to like fixing cars more than you like parting them out. Am I right?"

"You're right John. I can get my head into body work and forget any trouble I can dream up. I'll never forget after Sam showed me how to read metal and I ironed out the fender on that Ford and how well it turned out."

"That's what I'm getting at. Do you remember George Holcum?"

"Of course I do. He's the reason I was able to buy this shop, and now I do a lot of work for him."

"Well he's a banker like I am. And I like banking, but I have a passion for horses and buying businesses that are in trouble, and I make more money out of my hobbies, if you can call them that, than I do at banking. George has a passion for cars. I don't know of course, but I would bet that George also makes more from his hobby than he does from banking. When you sold him your Ford I would've held out for more money but you both seemed to be happy with the deal so I didn't say anything."

"Would you have bought the shop?" Jack asked.

"If it sat on the market long enough, and if I could have found someone like you to run it, I probably would have."

"You mean if you could have found someone like me and Gen?"

"All the better' but don't go selling yourself short. Is that Caddy you drive one of your fixer—uppers?"

"Yeah, but it wasn't nearly as far down as the Ford. Sam bought the Caddy to part out but it came with the shop and all I had to do was iron out the hood and one fender. I found the front bumper and grill at a yard on an old hearse they were parting out. The guy that wrecked it had kept it in pristine condition."

"Has George tried to buy it?"

"No. He's hinted at it a couple of times but never made an offer."

"I'm surprised. If you sold your Caddy, could you make more profit on it than if you just fixed it for someone else?"

"Oh gosh yes. Even if I sold it as a used car, let alone if I sold it as a classic."

"That's what I'm talking about. If you were more selective with the cars you buy, I think you could multiply your profits a lot. Of course that's my opinion."

"I could if I had the guts to price my cars like George does."

"Sure it might slow down your sales, but I think the wait could prove to be very profitable."

After everyone left, Jack told Gen about what John had advised.

A NEW DIRECTION

"Maybe we should give Daddy's suggestion a try. I can't think of anything it could hurt," Gen said.

"I don't see very many cars that I call classics, and when I do, the owners want too much for them or the cars would take an awful lot to fix them."

"How long did it take you to build the Ford?"

"Almost two years, working at least two hours a day."

"Let's put a pencil to that. Two hours a day for two years and some weekends, equals, let's say three months. Then we factor in an inexperienced boy compared to an excellent mechanic, about one-third, equals about a months work. And the profit equals, about five or six months pay at today's wages. I believe he made a pretty good point. We can go ahead with what we are doing, with a ready source of supply and demand, and while we are doing that, we can keep our eyes open for opportunity. We only have to find out what others call classics."

"All we have to do is read other people's minds? You do that will you?"

"Consider it done," Gen said.

On Saturday Gen told Jack she was going to go to garage sales and asked if he would like to come.

"Not my bag," Jack said.

She left and was back by noon. She found Jack in the shop cleaning up an old car. He enjoyed his work and spent a lot of his leasure time at what seemed to Gen as just more work. Gen understood his idea of fun so she let him run things the way he liked to. She would also keep him company as he worked. Gen thought Jack was just like John. Both of them liked what they were doing and seemed that working is all they really wanted to do.

"Look what I found," Gen said, holding up a stack of old auto magazines.

"Those are all out of date," Jack said.

"So are antiques, but they will give me an idea of what people like, these are not all I bought. I bought an old car."

"What kind of a car?" Jack asked.

"Just what we were talking about the other day, an old Oldsmobile."

"At a garage sale?"

"Yes at a garage sale. Actually they were settling an estate and they were practically giving things away to get it over with. Just get the wrecker. If it's not one you like I'll say I'm sorry. I only gave $200.00 for it."

"No, I know you are good at picking cars, it's just that I wouldn't have thought about looking for a car at a garage sale."

"You just don't like looking throgh other people's junk like I do."

Jack got the wrecker and Gen climbed in. She couldn't keep from smiling almost to the point of giggling.

When they got to the address, Gen led Jack around back to a detached garage. In the garage, was a car on four flat tires, with enough dust on it to grow grass—a 1951 Oldsmobile, Rocket 88. When Jack saw what it was and read the odometer he was more than surprised.

"Holy Cow! If you don't have the luck of the Irish."

Gen was so proud of her find she could burst.

Jack had to go back to the shop to get a tank of compressed air for the tires, but he got it to the shop that day. When they got the car cleaned up, it was a dark green with a cream colored top, it was what they had called a hard top. It had less than ten thousand miles on the odometer. It had been bought new by a man who died shortly thereafter but not before he had an accident. The man's wife had left it sitting in the garage and had never driven it. There was slight damage on the left front fender, that Jack smoothed it out like new. They ordered new wide whitewall tires from a specialty company and it was like a brand new car.

George Holcum brought a car by the shop. While he was there Jack showed him the Olds.

"What do you think I ought to ask for it?" Jack asked.

"If I had it, $35,000 wouldn't buy it. Of course if you'd take that, I'll write you a check."

"No, I think I'll try my luck," Jack said.

"I think I will just sit back and let you run. You seem to have the luck of the Irish at finding the bargains," Jack said to Gen.

"I just like to shop and spend money, and I don't care how hard I make you work," Gen laughed. Gen became addicted to reading about cars. She soon had the knowledge, but not Jack's skills. Gen's research proved to be invaluable she soon learned not only what cars were in vogue but how to price them. Between them both their abilities paid off in a big way. They seemed to find cars at every turn in the road and made more money than they thought possible. They bought most cars that were in need of repair, but also a lot of cars that people had only gotten tired of. And they were willing to sell under the car's value. But most of all Gen and Jack were having fun doing it. They enjoyed going to car shows and soon found out the best ways to market their cars. By word of mouth their reputation of being a ready market for people to get rid of cars that they felt were either to old or worn out. Gen knew which cars were in demand and jack knew what it would take to fix them up. When they sold the Olds and one more car that Jack had picked up, they had enough money in the bank to pay off the loan on the shop. It was a big thing to them. They went to see John at the bank and paid off the note on the shop.

NO MORE SALVAGE YARD

"By golly Jack, you seem to have the Midas touch. What are you going to do next?" John asked.

"I don't know about that but I know a banker that is good at suggesting ways to make more money. And I married a girl that always finds a way to make them happen."

"Like I keep telling you Jack, don't sell yourself short. But I think I'd probably take the salvage sign down and rename the business to something more in line with what it has turned into."

"I don't suppose you have a name in mind do you?"

"Didn't you tell me you married a girl who always found a way to make things happen?"

"By Golly! That's right," Jack said. Then he turned to Gen with the expression on his face of, "Go ahead. Come up with a suitable name."

"Why, 'Classics by Jack,'" Gen said with a big smile.

The next morning Gen was at a sign company picking out a suitable sign. Then she went over to Mable's place and asked her to come to supper that night.

"I invited Mable to supper tonight. Let's tell her about the name change. It seems like it should be something special," She told Jack.

"Sounds good. But let me tell her," Jack said.

As they were eating, Jack brought up the subject.

"How would you feel about not living next to a salvage yard any longer? We've decided to close the yard."

Mable couldn't believe what she was hearing. "Why Jack, I don't understand, you've loved that place since you were ten years old."

"We're not moving the place; we're just changing the name. Tell her what the new name is Gen."

"Classics by Jack," Gen said proudly.

"You scared me. You have the darnedest habit of just telling just part of your stories."

"I was about to tell you but you jumped to conclusions. We just like fixing cars instead of wrecking them. Oh, and by the way, I ran into Claude Colling today," Jack said.

"What did he have to say?"

"Not much. We talked about building on the knoll. He thought that was an excellent place to build since there was natural drainage, and it will be a beautiful home. I showed him Gens plans.

THE HOUSE ON THE KNOLL

About two weeks later, Gen woke up one morning because of a loud motor noise. She looked out the window and saw a bulldozer being unloaded up on the knoll. She slipped on her house shoes and went to the kitchen where Jack was starting breakfast.

"What's going on?"

"I'm frying bacon."

"You know what I mean. What's with the bulldozer?"

"That's Claude Colling, I told you I talked to him the other day."

"Did you sign a contract?"

"We shook hands. And with Claude, that's as iron clad of a contract as you can get."

"Jack, it's just like Mable said, you have the darnedest habit of not telling all your stories. Don't you need to go watch?"

"Claude said he could work off your drawings, but if you think you need to ramrod I don't think Claude would care. He knows how to build, and you can bet your boots he won't cut any corners. But you might start thinking about colors and decorating."

"I've thought about the house pretty often, but you seemed happy with the status quo, so I didn't say anything. Now I can't wait. I've been thinking of soft light colors and I'll tell Claude what I have in mind. Do you have any preferences? And are we on a budget for it?"

"Well, you know as well as I do that our bank account is fat enough, so we can build, and I thought we were both in agreement that was our plan. What ever color scheme you like will be alright with me."

"It just took me by surprise," Gen said.

Gen spent the next month spending money like the richest person alive. But she had everything bought and paid for well before they ran out of money. Gen spent almost as much time decorating as she did planning her wedding. She also cleaned up around the shop and it in no way resembled a salvage yard. It was now a showroom for some of their cars. Both she and Jack had sinking feelings when the truck from the scrap company hauled off the few remaining cars that had been bought for parts. But after a little mowing and planting some bushes the property turned into a virtual park. The barn that once held the motor blocks now was used to store cars.

LIFE CAN BE BEAUTIFUL

In two months their home was finished. It was beautiful. Gen got busy putting the fishing touches on the decorating and they had their open house party.

This time Gen did invite Margaret. Everyone was on time except Maurice.

Margaret said that he had to take care of some business at the court house and would be there as soon as he could. Maurice had been elected sheriff.

"I wonder how many votes his old man bought," John wondered. He also wondered why Maurice always seemed to be late for everything.

After a tour of the house, as Gen was serving refreshments, Mable said, "Claude still does good work."

Margaret said, "It's lovely."

John said, "Isn't that wall out of line?"

"Don't start up John. You know very well you're pleased. I'm so proud of you both," Mae said. She always seemed to know what John was about to say.

"Why the kids knew I was just putting them on," John said.

Maurice finally came in and joined in the conversation. "It's pretty nice but the location doesn't measure up to our division, Glory Heights. We have a very strict neighborhood covenant so no one can locate an undesirable building or business without approval of the neighborhood committee," commented Maurice. Then he started to extol on the virtues of presenting the appearance of prosperity. John butted in on Maurice's long winded try of making himself seem important.

"I'll be damned if I would buy a house where every damned snob in the place could tell me what to do on my own property.

What do you do when you want to plant a flower or paint your house, go kiss someone's ass and ask permission?" John asked.

"As long as it's in good taste the committee would permit it." Maurice said.

"Well, to each his own," John said. I just wonder how much of your prestige you can eat.

Missie enjoyed seeing Maurice told off. The only thing that bothered her was she thought, *That lap dog doesn't have sense enough to know when his intelligence has been insulted.*

John wondered how anyone on a sheriff"'s pay could buy a house that expensive. He also wondered why no one had ever been invited to see their house. *He must still be living off the fat of his old man's pocket book.* John thought.

"You've got every thing a girl could want," Missie said. And she thought, *With Jack.*

Gen thought, *"A baby would be nice."*

Jack was so proud of their accomplishments that he could have burst. Jack realized that his accomplishment were a direct result of Gen's help. He knew that without her help he would only be earning a meager wage. So he wanted for everyone to know. He asked for all their attention.

"Folks I am very proud of what Gen and I have done in getting this home and a profitable business but I want you all to know that Gen is the biggest blessing God ever blessed me with and without her love, labor and good sense it would not have happened".

Gen was embarrassed by Jack's praise but by the same token she was very heart warmed.

THINGS CAN CHANGE

Their fifth anniversary was approaching, and Mae wanted to have a supper to celebrate. She picked the Saturday before the anniversary for the date.

"I want to go to an auction on that date. They're selling a '47 Buick and I think we could make a bundle on it if I can get it. But I think I can go and still make the party," Jack said.

"We can tell them that I'm pregnant at the supper," Gen said.

"What! You're pregnant? When did that happen?"

"Don't you remember that night when you couldn't get to sleep?"

"Oh, that night," Jack said, going along with the joke.

"You better go see a doctor and get a checkup and make sure."

"It's confirmed. That's where I went this afternoon. Are you happy?"

"Well sure I'm happy, the only thing is, you're probably going to go through a lot of pain."

"I'd walk on hot coals to have a baby. It'll be like you and I will be one".

"You're going to have to quit working so hard."

"I'm doing what I like to do. It's not like I have to plow corn or something."

"You be careful anyway."

"Okay," Gen said. "I'll check with you before I do anything."

Gen had already told Mable of her suspicions but didn't want Jack to know until she was positive. Mable was overjoyed. She hugged Gen and of course she had to tell her all about how it would happen and how great children are.

The morning of the day the supper was to be held, Jack got up early. He told Gen he should be back in plenty of time for supper, and left. However he ran into difficulty and got started back late. He called Gen and told her to go ahead to Mae's and that he had called John. John said he could just pull his truck and trailer into the rear of the stables and it would be okay until the next day. This way he could be on time for supper. Gen went over to Mae's house and Margaret was already there, so they sat down in the living room to wait. Maurice was also late.

"Maurice is having to sort out some trouble at the court house. He's going to have a deputy bring him by later. I swear it doesn't seem they can do anything down there without his approval. And even at the country club, where we usually have dinner, Maurice is always swamped with other people's problems. Of course being sheriff is only a stepping stone in his career. He plans to run for the County Court then to commissioner and on up to probably the Governor's mansion".

Gen had heard all the dog and pony baloney she wanted to hear and said, "I'm going to take a carrot to babe."

Babe was a brood mare that Gen claimed as a pet. She went though the kitchen, got a carrot and told Mae where she was going. After Jack had put his truck in the stables, he came in through the kitchen.

"You just missed Gen," Mae said. "She took a carrot out to Babe."

"We must have missed each other," Jack said. "I want to show her the Buick."

Jack went back to the stables and was about to enter through the side door. He heard voices up by the front but couldn't tell what was being said. Then a shot rang out. He ran toward the front door and saw Maurice kneeling over a person lying on the floor. A deputy sheriff with his weapon drawn jumped in front of Jack and yelled, "Freeze!"

Maurice looked over his shoulder, and said, "Jack! Did you shoot Gen?"

Jack shoved the deputy aside, and saw that it was Gen.

"Oh no! Gen!" He knelt down and furiously felt for a pulse.

"Alright put your hands behind you," the deputy said.

"What the hell do you mean? I didn't do it!"

"I don't see anyone else. Put your hands back."

"You better do as he says," Maurice told Jack.

"You go to hell!" Jack said. And he slapped the gun from the deputie's hand and shoved him backward. Maurice jumped up and hit Jack from behind with his gun barrel and together he and Maurice wrestled Jack to the ground and cuffed him. When they had Jack subdued the deputy beat him with his fists while he was on the ground and then kicked him in the ribs and stomach. Jack was bleeding in his face and his ribs felt like they were broken.

The deputy went to his radio and called for assistance. Soon all hell broke loose. There was a swarm of police cars, all with their lights flashing, an ambulance and of course the family. A county detective told Jack he was under arrest, and read him his rights. Jack told the detectives that he didn't do it. But the detectives thought he did because of what Maurice, his deputy Woodrow, and Margaret had said.

"As we drove up, I heard a shot and ran into the stables. I saw the victim lying on the floor. My first impulse was to see if I could revive her. I got down and was seeing if I could do anything. I heard my deputy tell someone to freeze and I turned around and saw my deputy holding his weapon on the suspect. The suspect shoved my deputy aside and got down to be sure the victim was dead," Maurice told the detectives. He was belligerent and we had to use force to subdue him.

Woodrow's statements pretty well collaborated Maurice's statements.

"He's mean," said Margaret. "He once attacked my husband for no reason."

"She just don't like him because he beat up her lap dog boy friend," said Missie.

Missie's statement infuriated Margaret and Maurice. But to the detective it collaborated Margaret's statements.

Maurice and Woodrow were asked to come down to headquarters and make statements. Jack was taken away in handcuffs. The family was asked to remain at the house for further questions.

Jack was taken to jail and questioned all night. He was charged with murder mainly because the prosecutors always look at family members first and with the sheriff's and his deputy's statements the prosecution thought they had a pretty easy case. Jack could understand that he was considered a criminal. He thought that Maurice's statements were true, but totally because of only of what Maurice had seen. He had not seen anyone else there either but he was sure there had been someone else there. His only defence was to keep declaring his innosence.

"I know damned well that Jack is being railroaded," John said.

"Maurice only did what he had to do," Margaret said.

"Shut your damned mouth Margaret!" John ordered. Amid all the turmal and hurt John's temper was short and John was as much repulsed by anyone saying something good about Maurice as he was by someone saying something bad about Jack, And after he had seen how they had beaten Jack he was in no mood to listen to Margaret's praise of Maurice.

"Missie and Mae were both crying, but Missie turned to Margaret and blurted out, "Our sister has been killed and all you can think about is that lap dog. Why don't you go home and slobber on the bastard! He hasn't been anything but a pain in the ass since he first came around. What the hell was he doing in the stables anyway?"

"He went in because he heard the shot," Margaret said.

"The bastard thinks he walks on water, but he's so full of shit he would sink like a rock!"

Mae tried to quieten Missie but Missie wouldn't let go. Mae was afraid that Missie and Margaret would come to blows and she wasn't sure of what John would do. So she asked Margaret to leave. Mae tried to ask her to leave in a polite manner but Margaret left in a huff.

John tried all night to get in touch with an attorney who was reputed to be a very good defense lawyer. Finally, Bryant Stoddard returned John's call and John retained him to defend Jack. John didn't know if Mable had heard the news; he hoped not. So John drove over to Mable's house and as gently as possible he told her. Mable of course was very up set, but being Mable, she wanted to help. She asked John to take her to see Mae, and she rode back with him. After Mae and Mable cried together, Mable suggested that they go clean Jack's house.

"Oh, Mable I don't think I could, I know it needs to be done, but I just can't."

"I'll go with you," Missie said.

Margaret had returned to John's house, saying that Maurice had told her she should stay there until things cooled down.

"I'll go too. I need something to do. Let me call Maurice first so he will know where I am," Margaret said.

Margaret's car was behind Missie's so they took Margaret's car. When they got there, Mable and Missie started cleaning the kitchen, and Margaret said she would change the bed clothes. Mable thought they should take all the perishables and they put them in a grocery bag. Margaret put the dirty linens and all the soiled clothes she could find in a pillow slip and took them directly and put them in the trunk of her car.

"I've got to go by my house to get some stuff and I'll leave the sheets there and wash them later" Margaret said.

Mable asked Margaret to leave her at her at home. Then Mable got in her car and went to see jack. When she asked to see him she was told that only his lawyer was allowed to see him. She called Norman and John to see if she could get some help but they were also turned away.

Jack was held and no bail was allowed. Jack was not even allowed to attend Gen's funeral. Jack was allowed no visitors except his lawyer. Bryant told John that Jack's treatment was unprecedented but not illegal. The trial was set to begin in two months. Bryant asked for more time but his request was denied The trial started without delay. After the jury was seated opening statements were made. The first witness was the coroner who said Gen was killed by a single shot from a 9mm weapon.

Maurice and Woodrow gave rehearsed testimony. Jack's lawyer didn't cross question them. Except he questioned if either of the guns that were known to be in the stables were checked to see if either gun may have been the murder wepon. This question was suggested by John. Both Maurice's weapon and Woodrow's weapon had been fired for ballistic comparison and niether was a match with the bullet that killed Gen.

An insurance policy for $1,000,000 was presented as one motive. Margaret's testimony provided another motive. The policy was purchased because John had advised Jack and Gen to cover the shop when they had a lien on it. The premium was low and they had never canceled the policy. Margaret's testimony was biased and mostly untrue.

"My sister married a man with no scruples. His merits were that he drove a flashy car and had a smooth tongue. He promised my sister the world, but after he married her, he made her work in a junkyard, and at one time even made her live in a junkyard. Many of my friends complained to me about Jack harassing them for sexual favors. He even came on to me. He has a bad temper and one time he beat my husband for no reason."

Bryant objected that her testimony was hearsay, but was overruled by the judge. The prosecution also presented evidence that Jack had access to a 9mm weapon. The prosecution called John to the stand. John was sworn in. "We have evidence that you bought four 9mm pistols is that correct?"

"As far as it goes," John started.

"I asked you a yes or no question. Is that correct?"

"Yes."

"May I ask why?"

"Yes."

"Can you tell us why you bought the weapons?"

"Yes."

John's answers irritated the prosecutor, as John intended them to. Several people in the room laughed, even the judge found it amusing.

"Tell the court why you bought the weapons."

"Oh, I thought you wanted yes or no."

The judge admonished John. "This is a court of law. We found your answers amusing, but I think we've had enough. Tell the court why you bought the weapons."

"There had been a bank robbery locally and some bank official's family members had been kidnapped by robbers to force the bank officers into giving them money. I bought a gun for each of my daughters and one for my wife."

"Do you know where the weapons are?"

"All but one."

"The very one that killed your daughter?"

Bryant objected and the prosecutor withdrew the statement, but the idea had already been planted in the jury's mind. Bryant could not testify himself but to try to get the jury's mind off the missing gun he asked John if Jack's house had been searched. The house had been searched but after it had been cleaned. John knew that they had searched Jack's house but said he didn't know.

While John was on the stand, he testified that there had been some mischief in the stables and he thought Gen had confronted someone and was shot.

"It was something silly and I thought probably some kid had made a hole in the bales to hide in. But I noticed it had happened again when she was killed. I thought that it was one of the stable hand's kids, but it could have been someone else. We have a lot of people coming and going. It could have been one of the yard keepers or anyone."

The prosecutor's closing statements were that the defendant had motive and opportunity to commit the crime and evidence was presented that he would act violently.

Bryant's closing statement was, "The only thing for sure that my client could be found guilty of is being at the scene of the of the crime. No weapon was ever found. No real motive was presented. Not anything."

The case was given to the jury. Jack was found guilty. Bryant apologized to Jack and John, and he told them he thought Jack should have been cleared.

"With the judge's attitude we should have a good chance of appeal," he said.

"I'll get you some help," John said.

Actually John thought Bryant did a lackadaisical job of defending Jack, and he was determined to get someone better.

Max Arnold, a young attorney rented office space in the building that John owned. John had his bank on the first floor and rented out office space on upper floors. Max and John became acquainted and John ask Max to take the appeal.

GO TO JAIL

The verdict was returned and read. Jack was found guilty. Maurice and Margaret were happy. Mae wept. Mable and Missie clung together and cried openly. Jack was sent to the state prison. The sentence was 99 years.

Jack tried to be a good prisoner but trouble would often find him. When trouble did come he was able to take care of himself. Each day when visiting was allowed, Missie would drive Mable to the prison to visit him. With each visit, Jack could see that stress was taking it's toll on Mable. Mable was loosing weight rapidly and strength also. Missie began taking her food each day. The food was cooked by Mae, but usually went uneaten. Almost one year after Jack had been sent to prison, Missie found Mable dead.

Jack was allowed to go to Mable's funeral. The funeral had been arranged by Missie with Jack's instructions. Jack was escorted by two guards and had to wear leg irons. At the grave, people were allowed to shake his hand and offer their condolences. Missie though was one to push, and she grabbed Jack and hugged and kissed him before the guards could stop her.

On the next visiting day John and the attorney Max Arnold drove up to the prison with Missie. John introduced Jack to Max and Max told Jack that he had an appeal in the works, but it would take some time. Max had appealed the case on a miscarriage of justice. First because of the rush to prosicute then the judge had allowed Margaret's testimony to stand

As they were leaving many of the jail workers would tell Missie goodbye and say something like, "See you next week Missie."

Driving back, Max said, "You seem to know your way around that jail."

"I could bust him out of that hole if I wanted to," Missie said.

"Not a good idea though," Max advised. John thought that with very little encouragement Missie would try. Missie's visits to see Jack each week didn't stop. She didn't have Mable for an excuse to see Jack but she knew her reason for visiting him was because she was hoplessly in love with him.

Max kept working on Jack's appeal and almost a year later an appeal was granted. John put up $1,000,000 bail to get Jack released.

OUT FOR A WHILE

"Come on in and I'll take you to his office, Missie said. She took his arm and held it so close that they looked like a couple of newly weds. They went in and a lady sitting behind a desk looked over her reading glasses.

"May I help you?" she asked.

"I'm Jack Adams, I'm here to see Max Arnold."

"Go right in. He's expecting you."

Jack knocked and went in and Max motioned him to a chair.

"Can I offer you a cup of coffee?"

"I'd love a cup. I fixed some this morning but the grounds were two years old."

"I'll have to talk with Missie," Max said with a grin." She told me everything was ready."

Max poured Jack some coffee.

"Black okay?"

"That's fine, John said you could you fill me in? First I want to thank you for getting me out of jail."

"You're not out of jail. If you'll notice that ankle bracelet you're wearing. Now you'll be watched like a clock. There are a lot of people who are not happy about you're being out."

"Why is that?"

"Well first, there is professional jealousy. People don't like being told that they may have been wrong. Then, there are people who truly think you are guilty. And, if I know anything, there's some animosity toward you in the sheriff's office."

"Why the sheriff's office?"

"I can remember when you and Raymond punched a couple of them out."

"I'd almost forgot about that. Why do you remember it?"

"I was the kid that they were tormenting. I'll never forget it, and I'm here to tell you that Maurice and Woodrow will remember it to their dying day. Now don't do anything that may even look illegal. Don't drink, don't get in a fight, watch your driving, hell don't even spit on the sidewalk. If you are arrested do not, and I repeat do not resist but call me immediately. We'll have a different judge and jury, and I think I can pull some different stories from the witnesses. I know very well I can give a better summation than you got the last time. That's about all I can tell you so far, but I'll keep you informed about everything," Max said, and gave Jack his card.

"Keep this number in easy reach, and if you run into trouble, call me any time, day or night, Do you have any questions?"

"I can't think of anything right now, but thanks again."

Jack went by John's office to thank him for putting up his bail.

"Don't worry about it. The only way I could loose is if you run."

"I won't run," Jack said.

"I know you won't. So what are you going to do the rest of the day?"

"After what Max told me I think I should go home and hide under the bed."

"Naw, you can't do that but if you get time, you might move that junk out of my stables. Oops, I meant to say that beautiful Buick." John joked.

"Is that still there?"

"It hasn't been touched and your Caddy is in the garage. Oh, and Mae is expecting you for supper. Missie is waiting to take you anywhere you need to go."

MISSIE TAKES CHARGE

"Okay, I know you're hungry by now, and we're going to get some pancakes. And I don't want to hear that you don't want to waste the time again."

They stopped at a diner and Jack could not get over how much Missie looked and talked like Gen. She was not quite as tall as Gen had been, but she wore her hair the same way and she was full of life. She always had the same friendly expression on her face. She had matured drastically since jack had been imprisoned but Jack Still felt like she was a lot younger.

"Max told me that you kept my place up while I was locked up and I want to thank you for all you've done. Not only for that but for helping Ma and visiting me all the time. I don't know how I can ever repay you."

I could tell you a thousand ways, Missie thought. But didn't think that this was the proper time to liven up the conversation.

"You're welcome. I'm yours for the day. Where do you want to go first?"

"If you don't mind, I'd like to go to see Gen's grave. But stop at a floral shop, I want to buy some flowers," Jack said.

"There's a green house just before we get to the cemetery. Is that okay?"

"Fine," said Jack.

Jack bought a dozen red roses in a stick-in-the-ground vase. As they left the floral shop a sheriff's car pulled up behind them. They got to Gen's plot and there was only a temporary marker. Jack stuck the vase into the ground by the marker. When he got up he had tears streaming down his face. He had wanted to tell Gen how much he loved her and how much he missed her but didn't want to with missie watching. When Missie saw his tears and she knew he was hurting inside. She swelled up too and they cried on each others shoulders. Jack was crying for his loss of Gen. Missie was crying because of Jack's pain. But as they held one another Missie was experiencing some very inappropriate feelings. She hated the feelings but could do nothing about them. After they pulled themselves together, and they were leaving the cemetery Missie said, "We haven't gotten a headstone because we thought you should be the one to pick it out. Where to now? Do you want to go find a stone?"

"No, I don't feel like it right now,I guess back to your place, I told John that I would move the truck and trailer out of the stables." As they were driving back to John's place, the sheriffs car was behind them again.

Missie pulled up by the garage and Jack started for the stables. Missie followed keeping the chatter going all the way. "Are you going back to fixing up cars, now that you're out of jail?"

"I'm only out temporarily. Max said I'll have a new trial with a different judge and jury, but I could be found guilty again."

"That's a lot of crap. I think with Max defending you, you will be acquitted and the right person will go to jail. You know I kind of think that Maurice shot Gen or at least he might have some idea who did and just wanted you to go to jail."

"I don't know, I don't think he had any reason to kill Gen. Besides they test fired his gun and it didn't match the bullet that killed Gen. That came out in court. I was in the stables too and I didn't see anyone else. I think she probably caught some kid messing around and he had a gun and shot her before he thought about what he was doing.

"Maurice sure didn't like her. I know that for sure," Missie said.

"Why would he not like Gen? She was always nice to everyone."

Missie told Jack about the supper incident. "And boy he sure gets pissed off when you call him a lap dog and he's the biggest jerk that was ever borned. I'll sure testify for your defense and do anything else you need."

"You're a sweetheart. The truck was taking up a lot of room," Jack commented as they got to the stables.

"What did you say?"

"That's taking up a lot of room."

"No, what did you say before that?"

"You mean you're a sweetheart?"

"Yeah, that's it. I heard you the first time. I just wanted to hear it again. Daddy doesn't mind; there's plenty of room on either side to walk a horse through."

The stables were in a 80 ft. long and 40 ft. wide building, with a wide alley down the middle from end to end, high overhead doors at each end and a double swinging door half way down the side closest to their house. Jack had pulled his truck up about even with the swinging doors. Bales of hay were stacked to the side of the front door about half way across the first stall. The stall that babe was kept in.

NOT AGAIN

It took Jack about fifteen minutes to get the truck started as Missie stood and watched. He finally got it started and pulled it out through the stable and down the drive. Missie started for the house. As Jack got close to the road a sheriff's patrol car pulled in and blocked the drive. It was Woodrow, the deputy he knew all to well.

"Keep your hands where I can see 'em, and get out of the truck!" Woodrow yelled.

"What's the trouble?" Jack asked, as he got down from the truck.

"I'll ask the questions. Put your hands behind your back."

"Do not resist," Jack remembered and he obeyed the deputy's orders.

The deputy was cuffing Jack as Missie came down the drive.

"What's going on?" she asked.

"This don't concern you ma'am," said the deputy.

"There's a card in my shirt pocket Missie will you call call Max for me?"

Missie reached for the card and the deputy grabbed her wrist.

"Do you want to go in too?"

"Yeah, deputy dog. If you want some real trouble, take me in." Missie knew she wouldn't be arrested and wanted to show the deputy that she wasn't afraid of him. She absolutely couldn't stand anything about the sheriffs office and especially Maurice or his number one deputy.

He released his grip and Missie started for the house. She called over her shoulder, "I know who to call. Don't worry Jack."

Missie went in and called Max. She told Max what happened and Max started to the county jail.

The deputy roughly shoved Jack into the back seat of the patrol car and headed for the jail.

At the jail Woodrow yanked Jack from the car, took him inside and shoved him into a room with no windows and only a pull down bunk. Then he went to the phone and called Maurice.

"I got him Sheriff. Come on down."

Just as he hung up the phone, Max came in.

"You have arrested Jack Adams. I want to know the charges, and I want to see my client." Max said as he took a tape player from his pocket and turned it on.

"No recorders are allowed in here." Woodrow said.

"There's no law against the recorder. I demand you answer my question." Max demanded. Max was being as beligerant as he could from what he knew about Woodrow he felt Woodrow would be easily intimidated.

"Driving with an expired licensed and expired drivers licenses." Woodrow said. He opened the room to where Jack was still cuffed.

"I under stand he was on private property. Why did you think he needed arresting?"

"If I hadn't blocked him he would have been on the road."

"Where were you?" Max asked.

"I was barely inside the gate."

"Why that's trespassing. I'd better call John and see if he wants to press charges. Let's see, we already have a charge of false arrest, and, are you still selling drugs? Had you been stalking my client? Do you have orders to harass my client? Maybe we need to do some investigating. I think you may be violating Jack's civil rights." Max was asking questions faster than they could be answered and was confusing Woodrow.

All the color drained out of Woodrow's face.

"I demand that you release and unshackle my client." Max ordered, Max knew he had shaken Woodrow.

Woodrow was so shaken by Max's remarks that he took off the cuffs and told them they were free to go.

"Now get your asses out of here," Woodrow said. He was feeling foolish and he was trying to show that he was still in charge of everything.

"We'll go ahead filing charges against you for false arrest and trespassing." Max said as they left. He didn't think that he probably would press any charges but he wanted to give Woodrow something to worry about.

As they were leaving the lot Jack asked if Woodrow was really selling drugs.

"I've heard rumors but now I'm pretty sure," Max said. "Something like this is what I expected to happen. We now know for sure that the sheriff's office is out to get you. So a good idea is to keep someone with you as much as possible. You never know what they will try next. If someone is around, you'll have a witness. I just wanted to give Woodrow and probably the sheriff something to worry about when I told him I was going to press the charges."

Maurice came in shortly after Max had left with Jack.

"What have you got on the sap?" he asked Woodrow.

"I had to let him go." Said Woodrow sheepishly.

"You what! Why the hell did you let him go?" What did you arrest him for?"

"He was about to pull his truck out on the road and the licenes were expired. He got a lawyer, and the lawyer started talking about false arrest and stuff."

"You stupid shit head; that was lawyer talk."

"Then he started talking about pressing charges and asked me if I was still selling drugs. I got scared, Sheriff. When he left he said he was going to press charges against me."

"Selling drugs? What the hell did you tell him?"

"I didn't tell him nothing sheriff I almost had him."

"Almost and almost adds up to nothing, you dumb ass. What did you arrest him for?"

"He was about to pull his truck onto the road with expired license. I figured he would try to resist arrest and I'd have him good. But his stupid sister-in-law came out and I knew he would have a witness so I just arrested him for expired license. I'll get him good, next time."

Woodrow was making up the story about what he was thinking about resisting arrest. The truth was, Woodrow just wasn't thinking.

"There won't be a next time. I don't want you around him. If you see him coming you run and hide. I don't want you messing anything else up. The hay truck came in today and I've got to get the stuff. I don't need a lawyer nosing around right now. We'll have plenty of time later on. I want something criminal to charge him with and I'll figure out a good setup. You know as well as I do that he should still be in jail. You know he shot his wife. The bastard is just as guilty as sin."

Maurice was thinking. *My Father is finally proud of me. Everything I ever did was never good enough to suit him. When I played football he criticized me after every game. When I got elected sheriff he wanted me to know that he was the reason I was elected and he never spelled it out in so many words but until that junk yard dog was convicted he thought I had something to do with that bitch getting killed. Now that dambed junk yard dog is out and I'm not going to let him spoil it for me. If I can keep that stupid shit of a deputy from screwing up.*

Max told Jack that he had done the right thing, and he drove Jack back to John's place Then when Max got back to his office he wrote down everything that he had thought of that day. He thought of how stupid woodrow was and his mind flashed back to the day of the scuffle and he had to laugh when he thought of how stupid woodrow looked after Raymond had knocked him down. Then he thought of the look on woodrow's face when he mentioned drugs and how slow Woodrow was while trying to think on his feet. Max thought if he could get woodrow on the stand in Jack's up coming trial he probably could get him so confused that he would even admit that he committed the crime. He made a note that he could press charges but if he did it might give away something that he wanted to save for Jack's trial. Max was confident that he could win an innocent verdict in Jack's retrial case. There were so many questions that hadn't been asked. Questions like what was Maurices vantage point or was anyone else able to escape detection especially with the sheriff and his deputy wrestling Jack to the ground.

When Jack went in, Mae hugged him and kissed him on the cheek.

"I'm so glad for you to be out and I can see why you're upset, now you just relax. I still have some more fixing for supper. John will be home soon," Mae said.

Jack and Missie sat down in the living room and Missie kept the chatter going.

"Tomorrow, we'll go get the licensing fixed and I'll ride on the hood and thumb my nose at that deputy. I might even call him and tell him we're coming so he can find us, and maybe he will try something else stupid and we can get him locked up."

"I'd like to cause him some grief, but we better not try. I'll just stay out of his way and let Max do his job."

"What's the fun in that? If we can think of something, don't you think he deserves a little trouble? Maybe just making him feel silly would be fun."

"I'd like nothing better, but I'm skating on thin ice and something could backfire. Unless you can rig the jury for me." Jack joked. "So far as him feeling silly, Max has already taken care of that. You should have seen the look on his face when Max was firing questions at him."

When John got home, Jack told him about the ordeal and how it turned out.

"That Max is one smart cookie and I think there's something fishy about that sheriff's office. That damned Maurice hasn't got a licking bit of sense…And he will do his best to try to make people think he's a big shot. Why don't you just stay with us and you'll be where he can't bother you. And if either one of those bastards comes around causing trouble I'll dam sure press charges.

Margaret and Maurice came over. When they came in and margaret said.

"We didn't know you had company, we just came for a visit,"

"Why Jack's not company, he's family." John said.

It irritated Margaret that John thought of Jack as family but let it go. *That low brow is still kissing up to the folks and trying to worm his way in.* She thought. She knew why they were there. Maurice wanted her to find out if they were going to press charges against Woodrow. Maurice knew they would have proof because Woodrow had told him about the recorder.

"Everyone needs to stay for supper, I've got plenty for everyone," Mae yelled from the kitchen. Mae was like Mable had been, Mable's thought was that any situation called for food.

Jack was thinking, *They knew I would be here. They're here on a fact-finding operation. I'm* glad I can stay here. That lying bitcth acts friendly but I wouldn't tell her the time of day. And that damned Maurice I can't stand the thought of him even being alive and breathing up a lot of good air that some mangy dog could use.

They all sat down in the living room. Maurice started telling about a car that he had just bought. "Top of the line with every option available. I don't want anything but the best. Of course I got it worth the money by paying cash. You've got to know how to push your weight around and I've got pull with a lot of people. Those dealers know that if I buy a car from them that it's good advertising for themselves."

A rumble of thunder was heard and Maurice asked John if he could pull his new car into the front end of the stables since it might hail. John said it was okay and Maurice left.

Margaret was sitting in a chair across from Jack. Jack noticed that Margaret had a ring on her finger that looked a lot like Gen's ring. When Margaret noticed Jack looking at the ring she took her hand from the arm of the chair and held her hands in her lap covering the ring with her other hand. The quickness of her coverup convinced Jack that his suspicions were correct.

"Is that Gen's ring you have on?" Jack asked.

"Why yes it is. No one ever wore it and it's so beautiful. I didn't think you'd mind."

Actually no one else had noticed Margaret wearing the ring. She started wearing it without asking anyone and had become so accustomed to wearing it that she didn't even think about Jack noticing. No one in the family had said anything nor had looked at it closely. It was assumed that either Margaret or Maurice had bought it. Maurice had bought her a ring with a large stone, but it just didn't look right and Margaret had it appraised only to find out it was a fake stone. So she thought if she got Gen's ring no one would notice it. She thuoght she wouldn't be embarrased by it around the country club and she didn't think Jack would ever be around to miss it.

"I do mind," Jack said with a voice that showed his irritation.

"I don't want you wearing it. Take it off." He demanded.

It got deathly quiet. John, in an attempt to avoid a scene, said, "Jack why don't you pull your truck back into the other end of the stables then it will be out of the way."

Jack said no more about the ring, he realized that John was trying to put a stop to a sticky situation and was actually glad for John's intervention. Jack left and went out and started the truck. Missie heard the motor noise and suddenly remembered,

"I think some of the stable windows are open. I'd better go close them so the horses won't get spooked."

"I hope Jack don't step in some fresh horse-shit because Missie will step in it too," John laughed. He was trying to lighten the mood of the room.

Margaret took the ring and put it back where she had gotten it out of Mae's jewelry box. She was completely humiliated. If anyone had said anything else about it she would've lost all her composurer.

SAME SONG, SECOND VERSE

As Jack pulled into the alley way, he noticed Maurice's car at the other end. Maurice came down the alleyway and said, "Jack I want to apologize for that stupid deputy of mine. He got a little over zealous today."

"It's okay. No harm done." Jack said but was thinking. *Yeah you're apologizing but I'll bet you'd still have me in jail and giving me the third degree if Max wasn't around. I hope he doesn't start anything or I might just beat the hell out of him. It would be just like him to start something*

"I appreciate your understanding...Then we're square?" Maurice said.

Maurice stuck out his hand to shake and a plastic bag of white powder fell from under his jacket. Jack stooped to pick it up, and Maurice shoved him so hard he fell backwards into his truck's fender. Jack's first thought was.

"I'm going to be arrested again. What's in that bag? What is the matter with that bastard. Jack was wondering and his mind was going so fast that he really couldn't sort anything out.

You keep your damned hands off my stuff. Your nosy assed wife had to stick her damned nose into my business and now you, so get ready to get the same thing she got. Missie was coming toward the stables, and through the open door way she saw Maurice shove Jack and draw his gun. She also heard him threaten Jack. Missie was taken completely by surprise by what she was seeing and her reaction was one of desperation. Her adrenaline was running at one hundred percent. Someone had left a shovel standing by the door. Missie grabbed the shovel and as hard as she could, she swung it at Maurice's head. As she hit him he pulled the trigger. Jack was hit in the chest.

Missie grabbed up the sheriff's gun and pointed it at Maurice, and screamed, "Daddy, Help!"

"John was up and running. When he heard the shot, the first thought that came into his head was *Missie is down there*. As he was almost to the stables Maurice was getting up.

"Give me the gun Missie. You know you won't kill me." Maurice was telling Missie.

As Maurice reached for the gun a big right hand rolled into a fist hit him square in the face and knocked him down again. John took the gun from Missie and pointed it at Maurice. Maurice was struggling to get up.

"You son-of-a-bitch. You better stay down there, or I'll sure put a bullet in your ass," John told him. Maurice stayed down in a sitting position. He thought John would really shoot him.

Missie looked at Jack who was still standing but slowly sliding down the fender. She saw the red stain coming through his shirt and yelled, "Jack's been shot! That lap dog has shot Jack!"

Mae was almost to the stables and John told her to call for an ambulance and the state police. She went back to the house to call and came back with some kitchen towels.

A state trooper was the first to arrive. Then an ambulance. The trooper told John to drop the gun. Missie was kneeling down by Jack and holding her hand over the blood and trying to comfort him. Mae was kneeling next to Missie and trying to help.

"Who's gun is this?" the trooper asked John as he picked up the gun.

"It belongs to that bastard right there," John said and pointed at Maurice. "He shot my son."

The medics were giving Jack a shot to keep him from going into shock and told the trooper he was in bad shape and needed to go to the hospital. The trooper told them to take him. Missie climbed in the ambulance with Jack.

"Did you shoot his son?" the trooper asked Maurice.

"It was self defense. I'm the sheriff. He was about to attack me".

Maurice got up and the trooper asked him to put his hands behind his back and cuffed him.

"Why the hell are you cuffing me? I told you it was self defense." Maurice started to resist but thought the trooper could subdue him and he knew John would help the trooper.

"You admitted to the shooting, and until we get this straitened out the cuffs will remain." The trooper went to his car and asked for assistance. While the trooper was on his radio, John and Maurice were staring at each other. Niether of them spoke a word but the hatred was understood by both of them.

Margaret was the last to come to the stables. When she saw Maurice handcuffed and with a bloody nose and a small gash on his temple from Missie's blow she became outraged.

"You take those cuffs off my husband. He's the sheriff for Christ's sake."

Margaret was fighting mad and slapped the trooper hard across the face. The trooper grabbed her arm and cuffed her with a plastic tie. Soon the state detectives arrived. They noticed the bag that held the white powder, and a shakedown of Maurice produced two more bags. Because of
the suspicion of narcotics the FBI was notified.

Maurice kept telling the state police he was the sheriff and he had found the cocaine on Jack and he only shot Jack in self defense. He was talking so fast and furious he hardly made any sense and with his blabbering he was giving the detectives reason to doubt his veracity. He was actually giving the detectives information that could be used against him in court. One thing was Maurice's knowledge of what the powder was.

The detectives finaly sorted out what had happened and arrested Murice and Margaret. Maurice was arrested wirh charges of suspicion of attemted murder and Margaret for asulting an officer.

When everyone had left John and Mae both felt like things like this just don't happen and they both were nervous to the point of trembling. Mae brought John a cup of coffee and told John to take it out on the porch and light a cigar. Then she got herself a cup and came out and sat in the swing with him. They sat together for several minutes. No conversation was necessary they were just there for each other. After they calmed themselves, they decided what to do. John called Max and told him what had happened and Max told him he would see about Margaret. Then they both went to see about Missie and Jack. They found Missie in the emergency waiting room and found out that Jack's wound was serious but the doctors thought he would pull through. Missie told them then Missie broke down into uncontrollable sobs, The whole ordeal had been just more than she could stand. Mae hugged Missie close to comfort her. Mae understood that Missies toughness was merely a facade that she wore but underneath she had deeper feelings than could be imagined. Mae told Missie that she should come home and clean up and then get some rest. Missie reluctantly went home with John and Mae and showerd but afterward went back to the hospital.

The police came to the hospital to put a guard on Jack. Missie was glad for the guard. She didn't know if the guard was there because Jack was on parole or if they thought Jack might be in danger of farther retaliation. Missie told the police what she saw and heard and when the officers told the detectives, the detectives came and talked to Missie.

Finally after a night of questions, and investigation Maurice was booked for attempted murder and drug distribution. The detectives also searched Maurice's car and it was evident that Jack had interupted Maurice while he was getting the drugs from the hay bale.

Margaret was charged with conspiracy and assaulting a police officer. While the police were questioning Margaret, she realized how Maurice had manipulated her. From the police's questions she realized that Maurice had played her for a total fool. She told the police everything she knew about the crimes and the parts she had played. Margaret was realizing just how deep Maurice was in trouble and she was admitting some things that might cause her some trouble. When Max got there he advised Margaet to say no more and got her released on $10,000.00 bond put up by John. Then John took Margaret home to stay with himself and Mae. John asked Margaret if she thought Murice would try to harm her. He told her he would hire a body guard for her. Margaret didn't think it would be necessary.

Maurice was released on a $1,000,000 bond put up by his father.

IT ALL FITS

Jack was unconscious and in intensive care for three days. He had to have major surgery and was kept in a medically induced comma. The bullet had shattered one of his ribs and sent splinters into his lung. Missie stayed at the hospital most of that time. She stayed in the waiting room and went in to see Jack any time she could. When Jack regained consciousness, he was questioned and told the police what Maurice had said before he shot him. Maurice was not yet charged with murder because the prosecution wanted to gather more evidence and have an air tight case. Missie told the state detectives that all they had to do was see if the same gun that killed Gen was the gun that shot Jack.

"The gun that Jack was shot with happened to be the missing gun that John had purchased. It was not the gun that shot Gen." One of the detectives told Missie, and the detective also told Missie " if Maurice had shot Gen, he would have gotten rid of the gun he used unless he was a complete fool." When the FBI searched Maurice's home they found over $100,000 in mostly ones and fives, and they found another 9mm gun. The gun was found in a drawer and packed in a box that once held a shaving kit. They also found more dope, and Maurice's charge with drug distribution was enhanced.

Jack's recovery in the hospital was slow. He kept getting one infection after another. The doctors had to operate on him two more times. His time in the hospital was almost as miserable as being in jail he hated the confinement but his pain was so bad that even though they were keeping him sedated he had to lie almost motionless and the pain in his chest was a constant ache. From time to time in his sleep, he would try to turn himself and the pain in his rib cage would curse through him and waken him. Missie visited him every day and John and Mae visited him often. Missie's visits were the high point of his day. She was always so cheerful that sometimes she could even get him to laugh. Jack also hated the indignanty of having his bodily functions taken care of by the staff. The staff was very competant and professional but Jack still felt ill at ease. Even when he had an erotic dream his problem would need to be taken care of by someone else. When those dreams came along they sometimes featured Gen but it was usually Missie. His dreams of Missie caused him concern because he would have guilt feelings when that happened.

Margaret was staying with John and Mae. She had filed for devorce and Maurice didn't contest the devorce, so it was granted almost immediately. At supper one evening Margaret ask if some one would tell Jack how sorry she was about her testimony. She confessed that she had testified the way she did was because of what Maurice and Woodrow had told her. She also told them that she had taken the gun from Jack's house because Maurice said it was evidence against Jack.

"Please tell him that I was so confused that I believed everything that Maurice told me. I was in love with Maurice and thought he loved me now I know that he never loved me and only used me and I'm truly ashamed of myself."

"That's something you'll have to do for yourself Margaret. And you'll have to live with his answer," John said.

Missie thought, *Anyone who could believe anything that bastard said must be nuts.*

Margaret really felt guilty. It was a feeling that she had never felt before. She had thought that expressing the regret she felt to her family would ease her mind, but it didn't. She knew that John's show of wisdom at last night's supper was the proper thing to do. So she got up her nerve. She rehearsed in her mind what she was going to say to Jack. While she drove to the hospital she was fighting a battle with herself whether to go ahead with her apology or not. When she got to the hospital she sat in her car for a while and finally got up her nerve.

Margaret went to Jack's room, the door was open and he was sitting in a chair. He had just finished eating breakfast and the tray was still in front of him. He pushed the tray out of the way and was trying to get up but his weakness wouldn't let him get up without help.

"Please don't try to get up. I know I'm probably the last person you want to see, but please let me say what I came here to say. Then I'll leave you alone. I lied about you in court, and probably was the reason you were found guilty. At the time I thought you were guilty from what my husband and Woodrow had told me and I hated you. They even told me that you had been slipping around behind Gen's back. They had told me that some of the prostitutes they had arrested told them that you were a regular customer of their's. Since then I found out that I had been purposely mislead. I am truly ashamed for what I have done and for all the pain I have caused you. I came here to ask you to forgive me and forget it happened."

Jack was completely taken by surprise. He didn't know how to respond. He didn't like Margaret at all, but right then he felt sorry for her. He thought it must have taken a lot of courage and it took some time for him to think. He had never seen a more humble person than Margaret was at that moment. As Margaret started to leave Jack heard himself saying.

"No, wait!" Then after another pause. He finally sorted out what he wanted to say.

"Margaret, I've known that you resented me for a long time. I thought it was probably because I was not as rich as your family and didn't think I was good enough for Gen. Then John gave the impression that he favored me over Maurice and I'm sure you know of the bad blood between Maurice and me. You probably had other reasons too. I can forgive you, and I do forgive you. The forgetting thing will be more difficult. That will be as much up to you as up to me. The memory may fade in time, so let's not talk about it anymore. I know you are having troubles of your own with your divorce and everything."

"The divorce is already taken care of. But I surely want to thank you for listening to me and I can now see why Gen loved you. I have some other problems to work out, but come what may I'm glad you were so kind."

"Max told me that your testimony was the main reason that I was granted an appeal," Jack said. "As long as you have John, Mae and Max with you, you'll be fine."

"Jack you've been more kind and civil to me than I ever hoped you could. I admire you for it. I doubt that I can ever forgive myself but I hope to someday be your friend." It was all that she could do to keep her composure.

She left and understood that the past between her and Jack was over and she had a true respect for Jack. But still in her mind was the idea that no one could be that forgiving.

My God, he must be the politest person in the world. She thought.

At supper that night Margaret related how her apology went and what Jack had said.

"That's my boy, I think I'll adopt him," John said.

"No Daddy, that would make him my brother," Missie said.

"So?" said John.

Mae understood. Margaret also understood what Missie was thinking, and actually wished it would work out for her.

YOU AGAIN MAURICE

Then one morning, as Missie was waiting in the living room to ride to the bank with John when the door bell rang. Missie opened the door; it was Maurice. She told him she would get her daddy for him and tried to close the door. He held the door so Missie couldn't close it and shoved the door back open. Then he said.

"No Missie, it's you I want to talk to. Look Missie, I'm in a lot of trouble. Attempted murder is a very serious crime. I wasn't going to shoot Jack I was just afraid he was going to hit me. When you hit me the gun went off accidentally. You know that's how it happened don't you? I need for you to tell the police the truth. You know that I wouldn't want to kill Jack."

"Go sit on your daddy's lap," Missie said.

Maurice's temper flared and he hit her in the side of her face with his fist. John had just walked in and saw it. He hit Maurice in the face and knocked him into the door. Then John stepped into his office and came back pointing a double barreled shot gun at him.

"Get back Missie I'm going to blow this bastard in half," John said.

"John, you can't kill me, that would be murder. I just lost my temper. I won't do it again. Please John, don't shoot me!"

"I call it protecting my family. Why don't you draw your gun? Get back Missie."

"No Daddy! Don't kill him! He's not worth getting in trouble over."

Maurice was crying and begging john not to shoot him.

"Okay Missie, if you don't want me to. But you had better get your ass off my property before I change my mind". And then John pushed the gun forward as he would if he was about to shoot.

Maurice was whimpering and shot out the door and ran to his car.

"Were you really going to shoot him?" Missie asked.

"No, I didn't even have the gun loaded, but I scared the crap out of him didn't I?"

"I didn't smell any crap but did you see how fast he could run?" And Missie laughed.

"We better take you to a clinic and see if anything is broken," John told Missie.

They told Mae what had happened as she had been upstairs while it was going on. Then they went to a clinic. The doctor said nothing was broken, but Missie was sure going to have a shiner.

John called Max and together they went to the police and a warrant was issued for the re-arrest of Maurice. This time no bail was allowed.

When Missie came to see Jack he noticed her eye and became infuriated when she told him that Maurice had hit her.

"Wait until I get my strength back and I'll make that bastard wish he had never been born."

"I'd like that but Daddy has already taken care of that. Daddy probably broke his nose again and now he's back in jail and can't get out.

Jack was glad of what Missie told him but was disappointed that he wouldn't get to do the job. Missie's explanation of how funny Maurice looked when he was crying and then running was so vivid that she had Jack laughing out loud. Her manner of speech in mockery of Maurice's wimpering and her pantomiming of the way he ran was a comedy in ridiculousness.

MORE TROUBLE FOR MAURICE SR.

Ed Clark, an FBI man with whom John had became acquainted, came to John's office and asked John if he would wear a wire for the FBI. John agreed and asked who they wanted him to talk to.

"We don't want you to put yourself in danger, but if anyone connected to the sheriff's office or any of Maurice's friends come around, we would like you to switch on a pocket recorder."

Maurice Sr. came to John's office. When John's secretary buzzed John and told him who it was he turned on the recorder and told his secretary to send him in.

"Hi Maurice, what brings you here?"

"John, that boy of mine has me in a quandary. I can't get bail for him. I know how you would feel if one of yours was locked up and you couldn't do anything about it. Since you filed the last complaint against Maurice, the court won't allow bail. My lawyers have even stopped returning my calls.

"You might call Bryant Stoddard, I hear he's having trouble finding work since I canned his ass."

"I'm not joking, John, the only way I can get him released is if you drop the complaint. They might let me make his bail. I need you to drop the charges."

"Nothing doing," John said. "That shit-head came to my home and hurt my daughter and no telling what else he would try and if he came around again and caused more trouble I would probably have to kill him."

"Look we've been friends for a long time John. I'll scratch your back and you scratch mine. Didn't I pay off that loan for you? Now I'm asking for one small favor. Help me get my boy out I promise I'll keep him away from your house." In

Maurice's mind he had obligated john when John had collected Mable's money.

"Nothing doing," John said again.

"Look John, I tried to be civil but now let me lay it on the line. I have friends that will find it a real pleasure to mess up your daughter's face or burn you out."

"If you don't get out of here your face is going to get messed up," John growled.

"Okay John, you've been warned," Maurice Sr. said, and he left.

John called Ed and played the tape for him."That's great work John, it will open a lot of doors for us to look into some records. But I think we better get some people with special equipment to watch your house. Just having them around might discourage some unpleasant guests. Just tell your family so they will be on the look out and not be surprised with our men. His threat and mentioning his friends could mean that he has ties with a mob."

John told the family. Mae became terribly anxious. She was inside most of the time and hardly ever paid any attention to people coming and going outside. The stable hands and yard workers never had any dealings with her and she had just never thought about it.

"Do you think there will be trouble?" Mae asked. She was awfully upset.

"Those thugs don't worry me. If I can't handle them I'll call my daddy," said Missie.

"I don't think he will cause any trouble. Right now he thinks he is squeaky clean and if he causes any trouble it will give him away," Margaret said.

"I hope you're right Margaret, but let's keep our eyes open. If anybody sees some one strange, or some strange car or truck, let someone know about it. Especially you Margaret, if you see anyone that is chummy with Maurice or anyone connected to the sheriff"'s office, let someone know. I think we'll be alright but let's be careful," John said. "And Missie, I don't want you antagonizing anyone."

In truth John was worried but when the government men came and made themselves obvious he felt better.

GOOD WORK MISSIE

Missie was visiting Jack in the hospital when Max came in. She made it a habit to visit him each day at noon as well as most evenings.

"I didn't know you had company Jack. I just wanted you to know what we're doing on your defense. I don't think Missie will give away any secrets though. I'm trying to keep you from testifying in Maurice's trial. I believe what you said his remarks were before he shot you, but Maurice's jury might not. If you are sworn in, anything the defense might ask you or mess you up on, could possibly be used against you in your trial." Max said.

Missie spoke up and asked Max to see if he could get someone to compare a bullet from the other gun that they found in Maurice's house with Gen's bullet.

"The state police don't want to because they think Maurice wouldn't be dumb enough to keep the gun. But I think he is as stupid as they come, and I think it was the other gun they found at his house. I know for sure he hated Gen because she called him a lap dog in front of our family. And he still gets as mad as all get out when you call him a lap dog." Then Missie told Max the whole story about the supper incident and also what she had said to Maurice before he hit her.

"You may be right Missie. I'll see what I can do."

Max went to see the state police detective that was in charge of investigating Maurice's case.

He would do anything Missie asked him to with in reason. Max had a soft spot in his heart for Missie. He had thought about asking her out but thought she was Jack's girl friend. He actually had a crush on her. When Max ask the detective if he could get the comparison, the detective didn't think it was necessary.

"I think we have enough evidence already to bring murder charges against him, what with Jack Adams' testimony. I think we have a case, and the prosecutor is getting ready to charge him. Besides, do you think he would have been dumb enough to keep a murder weapon?" the detective asked.

"I think you may be right in the way you're thinking but even if the test proves that it wasn't that particular gun that killed Gen Adams, it wouldn't hinder the case against the sheriff. But I want to ask you to get the test done and at least not leave any stone unturned. I'm sure it will put a lot of minds at ease either way." Max also told the detective about the supper incident.

Max was able to get a comparison and it turned out that Missie was right. The gun found by the FBI in Maurice's house had killed Gen. When they did the test they found the ballistic test was a match.

The state trooper asked Max if he could believe the sheriff could be that stupid.

"I can now and I surely want to thank you. I can't believe he thought he had the gun hidden, but at least he was smart enough to use a different gun when they took the ballistic test after she was killed. But I think I can understand his thinking. He probably thought no one would be apt to find it and it had probably slipped his mind that it was still there until it was too late."

Consequently Maurice was charged with Gen's murder. After the prosecuter got the new evidence.

RECOVERY

Jack started to recover more rapidly. The doctor said the stress of his new trial had probably been greatly reduced and that helped in his recovery. Margaret's change toward him since the apology seemed to relieve him a lot too. Missie continued to visit him every day. Jack looked forward to her visits, and each day he thought about taking her in his arms. But he thought, *Missie is just being nice and wants to help just like she did by bringing my Ma to see me in prison. It would probably offend her to know how I really feel about her. She's so pretty and sweet and soft hearted.*

Raymond and Norman had been frequent visitors too. On one of Norman's visits Jack told him of Margaret's apology and how good it made him feel.

"You must have forgiven her," Norman said.

"How do you know that?" Jack asked.

"It's in the scriptures. Jesus taught us to turn the other cheek. And even in the Lord's Prayer it says, 'forgive us our debt as we forgive our debtors.' What you felt was a blessing from God."

"Then I forgive you too," Jack told Norman.

"What did I do to you that I need forgiveness for?" Norman asked.

"At the dinner we had when you first came here I saw Sam take a piece of gooseberry pie. I asked Sam if it was good and Sam said, ' Yes, Good and a little tart.' I started for the pie but you grabbed the last piece. But I forgive you."

"Well I'll tell you what Jack, I don't know if I can ever forgive you for not beating me to that pie, it was the sourest thing I ever put in my mouth. But I took it and felt obliged to eat it."

"I guess you're right about forgiveness Norman. I feel better already," Jack laughed.

"You know I'll bet Sam was watching and getting a good laugh," said Norman.

"*What Norman said sounded like what Sam would do,.* thought Jack and he had to laugh. Jack explained to Norman what was so funny and Norman was also amused.

Max gave Jack some good news. He had asked the judge that was handling Jack's trial to drop the charges against Jack. The judge said he could, but if only a formality of a trial was held the case could be completely put to rest. Max also got Jack's subpoena to testify at Maurice's trial canceled.

IT DOESN'T LOOK GOOD FOR MAURICE

Maurice was in big trouble. When his trial went to court he was charged with murder, attempted murder, drug distribution, assault and several other crimes, including evidence tampering and possession of stolen property. Even with a barrage of lawyers he had little chance of acquital.

Margaret turned state's evidence. She testified that she had hidden the missing gun and lied about things in Jack's trial. She testified that she knew when Maurice retrieved the drugs out of the bales of hay, but was told by Maurice that he was doing undercover work. She also testified that there was one room in their house she was forbidden to enter because Maurice had told her that there was police evidence in there that could be useless if tampered with. "I told a lie about Jack adams being a philanderer but at the time I thought it was the truth I had been told the tale by my husband." Margaret was embarrased during her testimony as she noticed several people that knew her sitting in the gallery but she thought.

Dammit I lied before and caused a lot of grief and that crazy ex of mine needs to know what to think of me and what I think of him.

Woodrow knew he would not get any help from anyone and in an effort to receive a lighter sentence in his upcoming trial also turned state's evidence. He told all about their drug operation and that Maurice was already in the stable when Gen was shot. He also told that Maurice Sr. was laundering money for them. Woodrow was being held for drug distribution and also as an accessory to murder. He thought Maurice Sr. should have posted bail for him as well as for Maurice. But no one made bail for him and he wasn't happy at all with the Fillmores.

When the state finished with the prosecution's evidence, the case looked hopeless for Maurice. He wanted to take the stand in his own defense. His lawyer told him it would be fool hardy but he insisted, and was sworn in.

"My mother, may God rest her soul, died of alcoholism when I was very young. I was bounced from one caretaker to another all through my childhood. In school I was constantly tormented by older and bigger children. If I reported the abuse I was labeled a trouble maker even by my father. I married my beautiful wife and we were starting a family. My wife lost our child."

He took a handkerchief from his pocket and wiped his eyes. "I'm sorry but it still hurts. We thought we had our lives back together and I was elected sheriff. I know it has been determined that the bullet that killed Gen Adams came from one of my weapons. I have given it a lot of thought and this is how it happened. As I was getting out of my car, my weapon fell out of it's holster and discharged. I heard the report but because of the echo, I thought the shot came from inside the stables. I picked up my weapon and ran into the stables, only to see my sister-in-law, that I loved dearly, lying on the floor. I instantly knelt down to see if I could revive her. I heard something behind me and saw my deputy holding a weapon on Jack Adams. Jack pushed past my deputy and knelt down and started feeling her neck for a pulse. I thought he was only making sure she was dead. I truthfully thought that her husband had shot her instead of an unfortunate accident as it was."

He recited the shooting of Jack in essence of the story he tried to get Missie to tell. Maurice really thought that he had the jury convinced and started to step down.

"I have a few question I'd like to ask, and remember you are still under oath," the prosecutor said.

"You can't make me testify against myself that's unconstitutional."

The judge told him that he was testifying by his own volition and he had to answer the prosecutor. "What the hell does volition mean?" Maurice asked.

"It means you will have to answer the prosecutor," the judge replied.

"I see that you are also charged with intimidation and assault. Can you explain that?"

"I just lost my temper for an instant."

"I see. Did Miss Harding say something to cause you to loose your temper?"

"She called me a lap dog."

"What is a lap dog supposed to mean?"

"Like I was a sissy and a coward."

"Who first called you a lap dog?"

"Gen Harding. You already know about that." Maurice was getting nervous and trying to outsmart the prosecutor.

"Did you think she was insinuating that you were a coward or a sissy?"

"Yes."

"She was just being hateful then, because you are no coward are you?"

"Hell no! I'm no coward. And yes she was a hateful nosy bitch."

"And when she saw you retrieving your merchandise, you knew she would cause you more trouble. And when you shot her that's all you could do. And she had it coming didn't she?"

"Yes!...No! I meant she seen me but I didn't shoot her."

Maurice suddenly realized the district attorney had tricked him into admitting murder. He started crying and said, "You got me so confused."

" And Jack Adams was just as bad?" the prosecutor suggested.

"Damned junk yard dog."

"I take that as a 'Yes'?"

"You're damn right. That bastard should be put to death. He deserves to die. Him with his damned boxing lessons and his kiss ass manners caused the whole damned problem. I never did one damned thing to him and he had to go beating me up and turning everybody against me."

Maurice was so mad and up set, he knew he was messing up but he wanted to say anything he could to blast Jack. In Maurice's mind all his troubles were a direct result of Jack and he thought that pure logic would convince people that he was a victim rather than a culprit.

The prosicutor had gotten Maurice to admit to everything. "I rest my case," the prosecutor said.

The jury took the case and in two hours brought back a guilty verdict, on all charges and a recommendation of death. When Maurice heard the verdict he yelled, "No! It's those damned junk yard dogs that need to be killed!"

Another date was set for the judge and jury to hear arguments either for or against the death penalty. Very few testified against the death penalty and those were people who were against the death penalty in general. Many people Such as prostitutes and merchants came forth with tales of Maurice being unethical and even threatening. The prostitutes although not confessing their trade told of being shaken down for sexual favors or cash. Business managers told of harassment to gain cuts on sales or service. Maurice had been coached by his lawyers that he should remain quiet during the testimonies but Maurice could not remain docile. He would often jump up and call someone a liar or worse and sometimes threaten people. His threats were empty but gave the indication that he had ties with a mob although Maurice had lost any help from organized crime and he knew it. After a week of testimony the judge sentenced Maurice to be put to death. He had heard enough testimony to convince him that Maurice was completely corrupt and he followed the juries' recommendation.

JACK GETS OFF THE HOOK

Jack was released from the hospital and had his hearing. His trial was held without a jury. He was deemed innocent by the judge. The prosecutor told the court that Jack was completely exonerated because of recent evidence revelations.

Jack moved back home but his mind was slower to heal. He had never felt so lonely in his life. He had his own shop, and tried to busy himself to relieve his loneliness, but without someone to work for and to be interested in what he was doing, it seemed fruitless. Also even though he had been released from the hospital he didn't have his strength back and he would tire easily and become discouraged. His despodency over Gen and Mable sent him into dark. depression from time to time. Raymond knew how Jack was Feeling and tried to cheer him up and was a frequent visitor. Raymond was more like a brother to Jack than a cousin and tried to think of ways to help him feel better. He asked Jack to go out with a lady he knew. She was a very attractive lady and pleasant to be around and gave Jack the impression that he could have his way with her. But Jack felt repulsed and broke off contact with her. So the relationship didn't work out. Jack was still grieving for his loss of Gen and never felt he even had an attraction to anyone nor did he want one. He would try to visualize loving someone else but it seemed imposible. In his mind he couldn't even put a face on his imaginary girls nor could he visualize holding someone other than Gen. However Missie did seemed to pop into his head frequently. A call from Missie suddenly got him to thinking about something besides being lonely.

He answered the phone and it was Missie. "Jack I've had an accident and I need some help."

"Are you hurt?" was Jack's first question.

"No I'm not hurt, but my car is torn up and will have to be towed in."

"Thank God you're not hurt. Tell me where you are."

"I'm at a gas station out on the highway at County Road H. A guy pulled out in front of me and I ran into the ditch."

"Okay, you just sit tight and I'll be right there." Jack got into the wrecker and drove to the spot. When he got there, Missie was standing by her car and looked as if she may have been crying. There was also a patrol car there with his lights flashing to warn other drivers.

"Oh thank God you're here. I didn't know what to do." Missie said.

"We've got it all under control now so just let me take care of it." Jack said. Then he took her by the shoulders and kissed her on the forehead. His calmness and kindness almost brought her to tears again. After he had it pulled out of the ditch he hooked the car up to pull it in.

"Hop up in here Missie an I'll give you a ride in my limo." Missie climbed up into the wrecker and Jack drove off to his shop. He backed the car into the shop and and looked at the damage. He could see that the damage was minor but it would take a few days work to put it back right.

"Looks like you're going to be without a car for a few days but it can be fixed easily enough."

"Can you fix it?" Missie asked.

"Boy, you sure know how to put a fellow down Missie. I thought you liked my work."

"I didn't mean to put you down…I'm sorry…I just didn't know if you had time."

"I know you didn't. I was just putting you on. Do you feel like driving home?"

"I don't think I could drive a wrecker."

"I wasn't going to have you take the wrecker. I've got other cars, but maybe I should take you. You still seem a little shaky."

While they were driving to John's place Missie thought, *I wish I could always have Jack this close. I always feel safe with him around. I wish I could tell him how much I love him."*

Jack thought, *I wish I could always have Missie this close. I'd love to put my arms around her and hold her close. If I ever could love anyone besides Gen it would be Missie."*

When they told Mae what had happened, Margaret was listening in. When Jack left Margaret walked out on the porch with him.

"Jack I don't want to butt into your business, but you seem to be trying to crawl into a cave. I think if you tried to have some fun you'd feel better. Come and see us more often or maybe go see a show with Missie or something." Margaret knew very well what Missie's feelings about Jack were and was trying to get Jack headed in Missie's direction.

"Yeah, you're probably right. I am kind of lonely most of the time. Thank you for caring." Jack said but he really didn't want any advice from Margaret. He felt more or less uncomfortable around Margaret and he never had completely made up his mind about just how he thought about her. He had developed a genuine affection for Missie. But he had a strange feeling about doing anything about it. He felt like he would be unfaithful to Gen. Try as he might, he couldn't get her out of his mind. He could find all the old cars that he wanted and his business was picking up again. But that just didn't seem to help with his loneliness. He started to work on Missie's car and somehow it made him feel good. He felt like he was doing something for someone else instead of just seeing how much money he could pile up. He had already rebuilt the Buick and hated every minute he spent on it. He felt like if he hadn't been off looking for it, he would have been with Gen and probably she wouldn't have gotten shot. When he had finished the Buick he just let George Holcum buy it for less than it was worth at wholesale, but still at a good profit. He just wanted to get it out of his sight. Both Jack and Mr. Holcum were happy with the deal. Jack also let Mr, Holcum buy his Caddy and Gen's Mustang. It seemed to him that if he got rid of things from the past at least they wouldn't keep reminding him of Gen. The sale of the cars also helped his finacial matters. He really didn't need to worry but thought until he got his business to going again a few dollars in the bank couldn't hurt anything. He felt like the business he was in would only be from deal to deal and thought it was what he wanted to do but if he needed to, he could still do repair work.

He would visit John and Mae frequently, but he knew Missie was the main draw. She was so sweet and friendly and it made him feel good to be around her. As far as he knew Missie wasn't going with anyone, but he thought she probably was. Missie would date some, but when she was with anyone else, she always was thinking of Jack. Her heart belonged to Jack. She loved Jack so much it hurt her and with his or her visits she tried to give every indication of her love. But couldn't bring herself to just come right out and tell Jack.

Jack wanted to buy a head stone for Gen's grave. He felt like the family should help pick out the stone and help with the epataph. When a suitable stone was decided on Jack ordered it and when it was placed at the grave, Jack, Mae and Missie all drove out to see it. Jack also took another bouquet. After he placed the flowers on her grave he couldn't help tearing up and they they all had a good cry.

Then as Jack was falling asleep that night and he was in the state of half asleep and half awake. He was startled by a voice that said, "Jack." The voice sounded like Gen. He sat up and saw Jim, Mable, Gen and Sam. Jim was in overalls. His Ma was in a print dress. Gen was in slacks and a wrinkle-free blouse. Sam was in coveralls with that glint in his eyes like he always had when he looked at Jack. Before Jack could focus his eyes they were gone. Jack was now wide awake. He thought it must have been a dream. But it was so real that he had a hard time going back to sleep. The next morning it was still on his mind. He was having coffee and thought, *I'll bet Sam got them all together just to let me know that they were all safe and happy in heaven. Jim was probably working with wood. Mable was probably taking care of Jim and helping everyone she could. Sam was watching everyone around him and enjoying himself. And Gen was making everyone happy and wishing she could make him happy again.*

BACK IN THE GAME

Jack made up his mind that he was going to try to make Missie fall in love with him. He thought Missie was real sweet to visit him in the hospital every day, but as it was obvious to everyone else he had no idea that she might be in love with him too.

He called the bank. He hoped she might be there as she was working for John as a gopher and learning the banking business. Missie didn't want to go to college. She wanted to follow in John's foot steps. John had not attended college but by reading and analizing people he became very successful. Missie thought John was the greatest man alive she loved being around him and thought if she could be like him she'd be happy,

Jack asked to speak to Melissa Harding. "This is Melissa. May I help you?" Missie said in her business voice.

"Hi, Missie. This is Jack. I was wondering if you had any plans for this evening. I'd like to take you out for supper."

Missie lost her business voice. "I'd love it. Where do you want to meet?" Missie asked.

"I thought I'd pick you up at your house about six if that's okay."

"You bet it's okay. I'll be looking forward to it."

Missie was all a twitter the rest of the day. John noticed and found it amusing. After they got home, Missie was still fussing around. She couldn't decide what to wear or where to wait for Jack. She dressed in a skirt and blouse. She kept wondering if it was really a date or if Jack was just being nice. She thought just in case, she wanted to look nice and yet not be obvious.

At six sharp Jack pulled into the drive in Missie's car. He had finished with the repairs and it was like a new car. Missie was ready but didn't run out to meet him as Gen had. Jack went in. John had a big grin on his face.

"Seems like we've played this game before," John said.

"No. We've already met," Jack grinned as he went along with John's joke,

As they left Missie saw her car all fixed up, she hugged his neck and thanked him. Then she thought, *Darn, he just wanted to bring my car back!*

"You're very welcome. If you have any more trouble you know who to call. Now do you want to drive or do you want me to?"

"For appearance sake why don't you," Missie said.

Jack went around to the passenger side and held the door for Missie.

They left and Jack asked Missie if she had any preference on a restaurant. "I don't eat out very often but I don't want to go to Daddy's favorite place."

"Where is that?"

"Elmer's Chili Barn," Missie said. "Daddy thinks that is the only place to eat and he always thinks it's a big deal when he takes us out to eat there."

"Aw shucks, that was where I was going to suggest" Jack teased. "There's a place over in midtown that Max said was nice how about there?"

"Sounds like a winner to me," Missie said.

They drove to the resturant and after jack parked he came around the car and opened the door for Missie and took her hand to help her out. The gesture confused Missie but she thought Jack was just teasing her. So she accepted his gallantry and went along, by thanking him and taking his arm.

It was a nice place. It was dimly lit. Jack was glad because he was afraid he would blush.

"I heard that Margaret was going to have her hearing today." Jack said as they were being seated. He was just trying to make conversation.

"Yes, but let's not talk about Margaret," Missie said.

"Okay, let's talk about you. I love you." Jack said as he sat down. He said I love you without thinking, it just seemed to pop out with out his planning for it to.

"What?" Missie's heart was fluttering and she could have melted. She couldn't have said anything else.

"I love you Missie, I have for some time, I don't know how you feel about me but I just had to tell you." Jack was glad the lights were dim and he felt like a blithering idiot. Missie regained her composure and said.

"How could you not know that I love you Jack?"

"You never said so."

"I've been in love with you ever since Gen dragged you in the house the first time. But I was afraid I would scare you off especially after Gen got shot."

"I don't scare easily, and you can say it anytime you want to. What do we do now?...Do you believe in long courtships?"

"I love you Jack. And I'm willing to do whatever you want as long as I can be with you. But...before we get married... if I can get you to propose.... I'd like to wait until Margaret gets out of jail".

"I love you Missie. Will you marry me?"

"Yes I will marry you Jack. I love you. I sure hoped you would propose." Missie giggled when she realiized that she had in reality did the proposing and was imbarrassed by her impulsivness.

"Margaret was sentenced to thirty-one days shock time for striking an officer, and seven years probation for her other offenses. Max convinced the judge that she was coerced by

Maurice to do the rest of the stuff. She told the judge she was ready and went right on to the county lockup."

"I'm sorry, I didn't know. So she's really in jail?"

"Yes she's really in jail but don't be sorry. Daddy said it was like slap on the wrist and if it wasn't for Max's ability as a lawyer it would have been a lot worse. Max convinced the judge that she had been coerced to testify the way she did and to hide Gen's gun and Max also told the judge that Margaret only slapped the patrolman. The judge said even the slitest touch constituted assault and he was bound by law to give jail time, but let's get back to you telling me you love me. I'll just sit here and listen as long as you like. Go ahead I'm listening."

"If I had any idea tonight would turn out like this, I would have bought you a ring and given it to you before you had a chance to change your mind." Jack felt like giggling or jumping up and down. A feeling of complete euphoria.

"I won't change my mind. And if it's all right with you, I'd love to have Gen's ring. It has Jack and Mable written all over it. I don't think Gen Would mind."

"No, I don't think Gen would mind. As a matter of fact I think she would want it that way. Do you want a new setting?"

"No I want it just the way it is."

"I'll get you a new wedding band since Gen's was left on her finger."

After they finished their meal that neither one of them was much interested in, they left. When they got to the car Jack asked if she wanted to do anything else.

"If you don't mind I'd like big long smooch." And smooch they did, as soon as they got in the car.

"You know this is the first time I ever kissed you and you kissed me back," Missie said.

"It won't happen again. Let's go someplace where we can talk."

Jack drove to his house and they sat on the porch. Very little conversation went on except an occasional, 'I love you' and a lot of laughter. After a while their passion was just about out of control.

"We better stop this or I'm going to have to marry you," Jack said.

"I don't care, I didn't think you thought I was sexy before this."

"I get this way sometimes but you know, I always thought you were really pretty and sweet. But I guess I had it in my mind that you were like my sister and I shouldn't have such ignoble thoughts. Besides I'm a lot older than you."

"You just get those sibling thoughts clear out of your head. I'll watch what you're doing, but you're right, I don't think we should open our presents before Christmas and you're not that much older than I am."

"I'm really looking forward to Christmas!" Jack laughed. "Let's go tell your folks".

When they got back to John and Mae's house they went in. Missie asked Mae where Gen's ring was.

"It's in my jewelry box in my bedroom. Margaret put it back."

"Jack needs it," Missie said.

Mae looked confused but left and brought it back, and handed it to Jack. Mae thought Jack was probably just wanting to keep it where he knew where it was and after Margaret's prank she didn't blame him. Missie was standing so close to jack that it looked like she was trying to push him. The big grin she had on her face was a dead give-a-way to John and he thought he knew what was going on.

Jack stirred up his courage and took the ring, Then he took Miisie's hand and said.

"John, Mae, with your blessings I would like to present this ring to Missie and ask for her hand in marriage." Mae grabbed Missie and again she did the dance then she turned to Jack and said.

"Jack I want a hug from you too."

"Well I wondered how long it was going to be before she got you to catch her. Congratulations Jack and welcome to the family again." John said ."But I don't want a hug just a hand shake."

"Thank you John…Gee I don't know why I'm so nervous… I'm glad that's over. Now Missie, will you drive me home?"

As they left, John walked out the door with them. "Oh I see, you got Missie's car fixed. How much do I owe you?" John asked.

"It's already taken care of a thousand times over," Jack said.

"Well thanks a lot," John said.

Missie drove Jack home. When they got back to Jack's house Missie walked to the door with him. She didn't go in but they kissed good night until they thought something else might happen.

Missie wanted Jack to go with her to tell Margaret. The next morning she was over at jack's house early. Jack had just gotten dressed but hadn't even had coffee. They drove to the jail and got permission to see Margaret. She was dressed in her jail dress, a dull, gray denim. The jail personel brought Margaret out of her cell and they were allowed to visit with her in the hallway. She was surprised to see Jack with Missie.

"Are you doing all right?" Jack asked. The thought of asking Margaret something like 'how do you like things in the big house' as a joke. But he knew it would sound insensitive. He thought that being in jail served her right. But there was no sense in opening old wounds.

"It's kind of scary but I keep my mouth shut and do what they say. It's really nice of you to come and visit me. This seems to be quite a turnaround with me being in the joint." Margaret tried to smile but she was feeling very embarrased and a little guilty at the same time.

"You'll be out in thirty days and that will pass before you know it." Missie said. "When you get out, I'd like for you to be my bridesmaid." Missie showed Margaret the ring.

"When didthis happen? Oh I'm so happy for you and Jack. I really hoped it would come to this, I can't think of anyone I'd rather see Missie marry. It is you that Missie is going to marry isn't it? I didn't even know you were going together. When did this all start?" Margaret was talking as though she was really happy about the situation as she really was and she hugged Missie and then patted Jack on the back. Jack was relieved that she didn't try to hug him too.

"We had a very short courtship of just about fifteen minutes. Didn't we Jack? Just don't go inviting any of your country club friends," Missie said.

Jack just nodded, he was really feeling uncomfortable around Margaret and didn't want to say anything that might stir up some unpleasant memories.

"Don't worry, they won't have anything to do with me. You can really find out who your friends are at a time like this. But I've also found out how to be a friend. You can't be a friend if your motive to be a friend is only to try to get something out of the friendship."

Jack thought Margaret must have had a talked with someone like Norman. The truth of the matter was, she had matured enough to listen to her mother. Ever since she had apologized to

Jack she was around Mae most of the time and they had many heartfelt conversations.

"We'll be back to see you again, I just wanted you to hear my news. You'll be alright just keep your chin up." Missie said as they were leaving.

"I'll try to Missie...Jack, thanks again for visiting me." Margaret said as they were leaving and she was thinking: *I never knew anyone so forgiving. He looks so much better now I guess the last time I saw him he was in coveralls and the time before that he looked terrible in the hospital.*

Jack just smiled and nodded as they left.

"Boy, I don't like being around a jail even if I'm not locked up." Jack remarked as they left.

After they had visited Margaret, Missie called John and told him she was going to take the rest of the day off. "Jack and I want to make plans about our wedding, so we're going to do some shopping and stuff."

She told Jack what she had told John. "What do we need to shop for?" Jack asked. "Do you want to go pick out a wedding band?"

"No I want you to pick that out by yourself. But first we need to find a place to eat breakfast, and I need some makeup so we will have to go to a drug store." They went to eat, and had a good breakfast, then they stopped at a drug store. Jack felt so good by being around Missie, that he was hoping Missie wasn't just ready to go home.

"Now where do you want to go?" Ask Jack.

"Why don't we go to your house and talk and just be together."

"That sounds like a good idea to me. I had a hard time going to sleep last night and some relaxation sounds great."

"You too? I had to keep turning the lights on to look at the ring and be sure I wasn't dreaming."

In the car driving to Jack's house Missie snuggled close to Jack kissed him every chance she got. She noticed that she was having an effect on Jack and snuggled closer. They got to the house and went in. They sat down on the coach and Jack pulled her close.

"I can tell you've gotten over thinking I'm your sister." Missie giggled.

"Yeah we better be careful just keep letting me hold you. When you would come to see me in the hospital, I would always think that if I could just wrap my arms around you and hold you close like this it would make all my pain go away but I was afraid I might be taking some unwelcome liberties."

"Jack you think deeper thoughts than I do. I always thought if I just crawled in bed with you we could have some fun, but I knew you were religious and I thought it would be against what your church teaches. You weren't the only one with those thoughts.

"Well, I'm just not sure exactly what I believe. I think the churches have a real purpose, and they are places to worship God. I really think that God gave us a conscience and it is up to God and to us to decide what is right or wrong. God is real and he will guide us if we let him. But what church doctrine is or what others think is of no consequence to us. If we try our best to do his will we will be blessed. And I think most preachers truly believe they are called by God to administer to people, and to preach the Gosple. But I think people have to do their own way of living. It seems to me that some preachers make up their own set of rules and some how convince whole congregations to abide by their proclamations and put down just about anything anyone does. Even to the point of telling you how you should dress or what you should think and

sometimes it seems to me that people get so hung up on some very small scripture that they base their whole concept of what God expects of us on that one small part of everything. Of course I suppose that we all have our faults and sometimes I think that my aggrivation with preachers is a sin. I certainly don't have wisdom enough to do any condemning."

"I hope God doesn't hold thoughts against us because I'm thinking the same thing you are.

"Can you think of anything we can do to get our minds off each other for a while? I want to just hold you and feel you're closeness." Jack had settled down somewhat by his thinking about God.

"I don't want to get you out of my mind either. but surely there is something we can do…I know what we can do. Let's drive around and see if we can find someone that is down on their luck and see if we can help. Maybe we can find one of those people that hold up the signs begging for money." Missie suggested.

"Why don't we go see Sarah. She is all alone and she might like some company," Jack said. "Besides I want to show you off. I want everyone in the world to know that I've gotten you to love me."

He hadn't thought about Sarah in a long time, and he thought that Sam would smile down from heaven if he could give Sarah some sort of pleasure. He was sure in his mind that Sam was the reason he had gotten so close to Missie and made him as happy as he was right now and he just had to tell someone.

Missie was swimming in pure glory herself. She too wanted to shout it from the roof tops.

They drove over to Sarah's place and knocked on her door. Sarah opened the door and when she saw Jack she didn't recognize him immediately.

"Hi Sarah. How're you doing?" Jack asked.

"Well as I live and breathe, Jack Adams. I haven't seen you since Mable died. I'm so sorry for your losses. Are you doing alright?"

"I'm doing okay. I brought someone over for you to meet. This is my soon to be wife Missie Harding."

Sarah squinted passed Jack and saw Missie.

"Well you're a pretty thing. I didn't know if Jack would ever get married again. Come on in and let's get acquainted. I met you when you drove me to the bank I think."

They went in and immediately Missie and Sarah started talking like old friends. Sarah reminisced about how she and Sam started out and how she always wanted a daughter and Sam always wanted a boy. Missie noticed the hurt in her eyes and went over and knelt before her and took both of Sarah's hands and at that moment a friendship was born. When Jack and Missie left each of them was in a different mood. But still they didn't seem to be able to let go of each other.

Then jack wanted to go by Raymonds house and let his Aunt June know.

From that day on Jack was no longer lonesome.

As they were leaving, Jack was thinking. *I wish my folks, Gen and Sam weres still around and I know they would be happy for me.*

Missie didn't want a big wedding. She said she just wanted it to happen before Jack changed his mind.

"Then, I'll have you hogtied and henpecked before you know what happened," She told Jack.

"Why I'll have you pregnant and barefoot, before you know what happened," Jack came back.

"Promises, promises. You don't scare me," Missie giggled.

Mae said that even if Missie did want a small wedding she would like to have a nice reception. So it was agree, just family and close friends. Missie's only formal thing she wanted was for John to give her hand to Jack. She had thought that his giving Gen's hand to Jack was really a nice part of the ceremony.

"I don't know if I can just give you away. Let's see if I can sell you first. I might be able to get a camel and a couple of goats for you," John teased. "I'm not just loosing a daughter but also a good gopher.

"You drive a hard bargain John, I don't know where I can find a camel." Jack said "but I think I can get you a whole herd of goats." Jack went along with John's joke.

Mae wanted it to be a big day for Missie anyway. She tried to get Missie to plan a more elaborate wedding. But to Missie it was just something to get out of the way before she could just be Mrs. Jack Adams. Mae did get her to buy a nice dress. It was a lace dress but not a gown. Mae said at least Missie wouldn't wear jeans. Missie told Jack to just wear a suit. "Momma will faint if you show up in your coveralls."

Mae got Missie to send invitations. But Missie insisted to only have the wedding in the living room of the house. When the guests arrived Mae came ddown the stairs and took her seat then John with Missie came down. They stopped in front of Norman and as he had been instructed Norman asked who gives this woman to be married. Her mother and I John said and gave her hand to Jack. Then Norman performed the wedding and of course Raymond was Jack's best man. Mae put together a reception that was like a dinner party. She had table space for everyone and food to suit any taste plus a big wedding cake.

IT DOES MEAN JACK

After the reception Jack and Missie went home to the house on the knoll. At noon the next day they finally woke up as it had been after four o'clock in the morning before they went to sleep.

COOKING LESSONS

"Where do you want to go for breakfast?" Missie asked.

"Just look in the refrigerator and fix what you want." Jack said.

Missie looked in the refrigerator and panicked. "Jack there's something I need to tell you. I don't know how to cook anything."

Jack found it hard to believe, but when he saw the bewildered look on Missie's face he knew it was so. Then he said.

"Okay, it's not the end of the world. I've done breakfast by myself for a long time."

He set a skillet on the stove and turned around and started the coffee. When he thought the skillet was hot enough and he peeled off the bacon and put it into the skillet. Next he put a skillet on another burner and put some butter in that skillet.

"That butter should melt quick enough to start the eggs and they should be done when the bacon is done," he said. "Now put some bread in the toaster and get the plates and we're ready to eat."

"What else are you good at?" Missie asked.

"I thought I showed you that last night."

"Yes. That was quite a talent. But I'm talking about cooking. let's get back to cooking. I think I can handle supper."

Missie had been around John enough and watched him charbroil steaks she knew she could do that for supper. But she knew she wouldn't know how to cook regular meals. The next morning, Missie was up and had breakfast ready when Jack got up. "You're a fast learner," Jack said.

"I can do breakfast now but I'll have to go over and ask Momma how to cook everything else."

She's a good cook but I never paid any attention while she was cooking, except she would let me make cookies sometimes. I don't guess you would like to only eat cookies the rest of your life, would you?" Missie teased.

When Missie told Mae what she wanted Mae didn't give her much information.

"Why honey, I can't teach you how to cook in one easy lesson. It'll take months," Mae said. "You'll just have to learn it on your own. Just get you a good cook book and follow the recipes."

Margaret was listening in. "You don't need to know how to cook, all you need to know is how to fake it. Let's go shopping."

As they got into Missie's car, Margaret started giving instructions, "First, stop at a book store, and we'll get some cookbooks. We'll just get two. A "Dummies" book and a Betty Crocker. Then to the grocery store. What do you want to cook?"

"Jack likes fried chicken," Missie said.

"That's a hard one; but let's start off with the chicken. We won't buy a whole chicken; we'll buy it in parts. Then we need some lard, but most people use Crisco now. So let's get a can, and some flour to roll the chicken in. It'll tell you in the book how to do it. You'll want some mashed potatoes and gravy? Let's go over here. There see that box of instant mashed potatoes? Get a box. All you have to do is boil some water, and then just follow the instructions on the box. What else do you want?"

"With mashed potatoes, I've got to have gravy."

"Gravy comes in a jar or a pouch. I usually use the jars, because all you have to do is heat it up. But you'll have to learn to make gravy. The stuff that is ready made will do in a pinch but you'll find out that it's real easy to make. They sell salad already cut up and table ready and rolls that you only need to heat them up."

"I know that they sell vegetables in cans," Missie said.

"They do. But look over here, these vegetables come in plastic bags. They're frozen and they taste better I think. All you need to do is boil them in water bag and all, and put some salt and butter on them when you dump them in a bowl."

"What do you do for dessert? Do they sell pies here too?" Missie asked.

"I don't like factory pies. I usually pick them up at that little cafe on Main Street. They're fresh baked. I can tell you a secret. The pies that Daddy always brags about are the pies that come from there."

"You mean that Momma cheats?" Missie was surprised.

"Where do you think I got the idea? It's not cheating; it's just cooking the easiest way. If you really want to cheat, you can even get the chicken at a deli. You see you don't have to know how to cook, you only have to know how to shop. When you're in a grocery just look around and read instructions on the lables and in no time you can set up a meal.

At supper that evening, Jack made the remark, "I thought you said that you didn't know how to cook."

"Margaret taught me how and with a little practice I think I can become a real gourmet. But I need you to be honest though, and let me know what you like and what you hope I never fix again. By the way, do you like chili? Daddy taught me how to cook that years ago."

"One of my favorite meals," Jack said. "You'll do fine, as sweet as you are I'll bet if you only served slop, it would be delicious.

Missie knew Jack would not complain about her cooking but she also knew that she was going to learn how to be an excellent cook and home maker. She studied her cook books and soon learned how and no one had anything to complain about.

THE HONEYMOON

"Where are we going to honeymoon?" Jack asked Missie.

"Do you have somewhere in mind? I've never given it any thought. I always thought a honeymoon was just to learn about sex and we've got that down pat. I just thgought how wonderful it will be just to be alone with you and be happy."

"Yeah, you're right, and I am happy to be with you. I do enjoy having sex, but I want to do some things that we will have fun doing and travel is one of those things. I've thought about going to the Southwest. I read a lot of western cowboy books when I was young and I think I'd like to see the deserts and the mountains. Does that sound good to you?"

"Any place you want to go is good with me. I've been to Culverstone and that's about all I know of travel. Except I know where the prison is located and I sure don't want to go back there!"

Jack went to a travel agency and had an itinerary drawn up. He had it fixed so they would only travel up to four hours before there would be something interesting to see or do. He made all the reservations for places to stay overnight. He showed the plan to Missie and she became anxious to go. Their trip was planned for late spring so they would probably have good weather. The trip overwhelmed Missie, and she loved every day of it. They saw the prairies and the Grand Canyon and everything interesting along the way. Of course Jack wanted to see every historical place they came across. Jack also enjoyed the scenery. But he especially kept noticing along the way it seemed that people never got rid of their old cars. He was thinking he might some day take this same trip in a truck and load up some cars that he could love back to health. Parked by an old barn he noticed a 1940 ford that a person could see

IT DOES MEAN JACK

had not been touched for years and he made a mental note of where it was.

They took in all the interesting points on the way out and Missie loved the beach. She did wonder though why the people out there wore so little clothes and thought that people looked rediculous with their butts hanging out as she desribed them. They drove on up to Frisco, and took in China Town and ate Chinese food. The next morning Missie woke up sick. They thought the food just probably didn't agree with her, but after a week of being sick each morning, Missie had a pretty good idea of what was wrong.

"Jack, please don't throw my shoes away."

"What are you talking about? Why would I throw your shoes away?"

"You said you were going to have me pregnant and barefooted and now I know you weren't kidding."

"You think you're going to have a baby? Are you sure? Are you glad?" Jack exclaimed.

"I'm pretty sure, and I'm very glad. But please don't throw my shoes away."

"Okay. You can keep your shoes," Jack laughed" And I hope you know what you're talking about." Jack was really more than happy but he had the same feelings that he had when Gen told him she was pregnant. More concerned for Missie than he wanted to feel.

Missie could hardly wait to get back and tell Mae.

"How was the trip?" Mae asked.

"I don't know. I started having morning sickness," Missie giggled. She knew the news was going to be a shock to Mae.

"You started having morning sickness? Oh my God are you pregnant?"

"I think so."

Mae was overjoyed. She immediately started making plans. Her first grandchild had miscarried and her second died without being born.

"How can I help? Do you need any help with anything? House keeping, cooking or anything? I can come and help you when you have your baby and of course we need to get a crib and everything. Let's go shopping. There's so many things we need to do."

"No, I think I can handle everything since Margaret taught me how to boil water and how to open cans. I'll be fine. I think we'll have plenty of time to get everything else done."

"Margaret has moved to Culverstone. She said she wants to start over. She has an apartment of her own and is working as a secretary to a business owner. I think she's going to be alright now. But she won't be here for you. So anything you need or want you ask me." Mae told her.

"I hope she gets it all together." She has a level head. I found that out when she taught me how to cook." Missie said.

AND NOW

Time has passed—Missie and Jack have a fine son that they named John and are happy together. Jack still buys and restores old cars and is very prosperous doing so. They have no money problems. Jack came into so much money after everything was settled. The insurance policy paid double indemnity as the murder was deemed accidental death. And Mable's estate was left practically intact. But Jack considered the insurance and Mable's estate blood money and really hated having to spend any of it. He did have a lot of legal fees to settle though and he made sure that John and his attorneys were repaid in full. He also had a huge medical bill to settle. His medical bill was over $2,000,000.00 However Max helped him with that. Max had an accountant go through his bills and look for exorbitance and errors, of which there were many, and he also pointed out in his brief that some of the infections that Jack had suffered could have been caused by germs that came only from the hospital. Jack's bill was reduced to a reasonable price. Jack paid only a fraction of the original bill. But after all his bills were settled he had used practically all his inheritance except he still owned Mable's house. Jack earns more than enough money with his auto business to live a luxurious life but he likes to do things that have nothing to do with making money. He lives and breathes for his son and always lets him have first pick at the table and always finds time to play with him. He also counts Missie as one of his greatest blessing. He loved Gen with all his heart. But Missie has a way to keep his life free and easy. She is her own person and never worries about what others may think of her and never worries about what anyone does or what they have. She keeps her house in order and always fixes nourishing meals. She learned to be a good cook and says she wouldn't think of cooking out of a can but she giggles when she says it. Also with her easy and loving ways she keeps their home cheerful and comfortable.

Missie is still happy and in love with Jack. She loves the life of wife and mother and is somewhat involved with Jack in his business. She likes to go with him to auctions and always takes their son when she goes. She caught the traveling bug when they went on their honeymoon and insists on a vacation trip each year which Jack enjoys also. She started going to church and is on a committee that visit the sick and infirm. She mainly drives older persons who have no other way of getting around to do their shopping or to see their doctors. Sam's wife Sarah is her favorite person to help and Sarah thinks of Missie as her daughter. Hardly a day passes that she doesn't find someone in need and works diligently to solve problems that she discovers. She has developed a love for cars and says it's like getting a new car each time Jack gets one finished. The biggest problem they have is Missie picking out cars that are not necessarily classics or some that take a lot of repair. But Jack usually lets her have her way. Her favorite car at this time is a 1957 Ford with a Continental kit on the back. It has a factory flaw that was built in. It has an oil restriction between the motor block and the heads. But Jack can keep it fixed. Missie feels as though she married the most wonderful man in the world and after her Daddy, the smartest man in the world. She does tease him about his taste in transportation though, Jack's favorite car is the 1940 Ford convertible that he had noticed when they were on their honeymoon. Jack and Missie drove over to buy it and brought it back. The buying of the car was a real lesson in guilding the lilly. When Jack knocked on the door and asked the man about buying it, the man thought he had a big fish on the line.

"Well I reckon I might sell it but I'd have to get $1,000 for it" the man said. "It's in good shape I only quit driving it because I would have had to put turn signals on it to get it to pass inspection. It needs a little cleaning up, but if you put a battery in it I figure you could drive her home". Missie couldn't believe Jack could be gullible enough to believe the story but held her tounge. Jack was not taken in by the sales pitch but he looked the car over to make sure it could be restored. As they drove off with Jack's prize Missie could hold it in no longer and started razzing Jack.

"I'm glad he didn't sell you the whole State of Oklahoma. He didn't tell you a word of truth".

"I guess you're right but what he didn't know is how much I would have paid for the car."

"How much will you make after you get it fixed?" Missie asked.

"I won't sell it, I don't think even John would have enough money to buy it."

When Jack had the car finished it only looked like a 1940 Ford. He was very careful to keep it looking original but underneath was all new and modern running gears including power steering, air conditioning, turn signals and all the other things to make it up to date.

John and Mae still live on their horse ranch and love it. John is still busy with his banking and Mae busies herself giving dinner parties for any reason she can think of, and of course she does quite a bit of baby sitting. She fixed up one of her rooms so she can keep her grandsons overnight. The grandsons like to visit for no reason at all. They love their silly old grandpa as Mae has dubbed John.

Margaret fell in love with her employer. The owner of "JOE'S SCRAP METALS," David McCurey. They were married and they too have a son. They live in a beautiful home that sits next door to their business. The location of their home was Margaret's idea. Margaret wanted to show the world and her family that she was her own person and didn't need to pretend for anyone's benefit or for their acceptance.

Maurice is still on death row waiting for appeal after appeal by groups that consider the death penalty unconstutional. Not a day goes by that he doesn't spend his time hating the world and especially Jack and Gen.

Woodrow Carmichael is in the state prison serving a fifteen year sentence for drug distribution plus a consecutive sentence of thirty years for his part in Gen's murder. He thinks that Maurice and Maurice Sr. set him up to take the fall. He hates just about everyone and is miserable remembering all the things that has happened to him.

Maurice Sr. was convicted of money laundering, tax evasion, and racketeering. He was sentenced to sixty years in federal prison, but took his own life before going to prison. In the note that he left, he blamed his son for the disgrace the he couldn't live with.

ONE MORE LESSON IN FORGIVENESS

A news report came out. It read in essence, Convicted killer Maurice Fillmore, after loosing his last appeal, has told the press, "I have found the Lord and I have found his salvation. Jesus has forgiven me of my sins, and if I must be put to death, I shall rest in peace. I ask the ones that I have harmed by taking their loveone's life for their forgiveness also."

Jack read the article and was touched. He knew how much Margaret's apology had meant to him, and he also knew that Maurice had a justifiable reason for not liking him. He knew why Maurice hated him for a fact. He did have trouble understanding how big a thing Maurice had made of one little scrap.

"Do you think we should tell him we forgive him?" Jack asked Missie.

"I'd forgive him alright, if they'd let me pull the switch and I could stand where he could see who was doing the pulling."

John had a different slant on it than did either Missie or Jack. "It seems to me that just about everyone that is about to die gets religious after there is no other way out. I think Maurice is grasping at straws and hoping to garner public support and put pressure on officials to possibly grant him some sort of a reprieve."

"I think it would be the Christian thing to do," Mae said.

Norman is the one I should ask, Jack thought.

"Probably a forgiving spirit is in order. If you feel it in you heart to forgive him I say you should," Norman said.

"I think I should," Jack said, "When and if I can see him, will you go with me?"

"I will be glad to," Norman replied.

Norman and Jack drove to the prison, and after a lot of red tape they were allowed a visit. "What the hell do you want? Are you here to see all the trouble you caused me and to brag?"

Maurice looked terrible. He had lost so much weight that his ashen gray skin just hanged in wrinkles and his hair was completely gray and very thin. His eyes were sunken back in his face, and around his eyes the skin was nearly black.

"No, I came to let you know that I forgive you and to ask your forgiveness for the harm that I have caused you."

"Forgive you? Why you low down piece of shit, you ain't nothing but a G.d…. junk yard dog and I hope you rot in hell. And I hope your damnbed preacher friend goes with you."

Jack and Norman turned and left, and as they walked out Maurice was still cursing and calling Jack everything he could think of. "You son-of-a-bitch. You cost me everything I own, you bastard. I've got friends and I'll see your ass dead before you get me killed."

"I'm sorry Norman; that didn't go like I hoped."

"You don't have anything to be sorry about. You tried to do the right thing… You did, do the right thing. Now you can start forgetting about it. He is about the maddest person I've ever seen and he's going through his own personal hell right now. I'm going to pray for him and ask Jesus to ease his mind and perhaps he can find true redemption."

"That is a load off my mind, and I think you're right Norman. Thanks for coming with me."

Jack had hoped his apology would make Maurice feel better but it had the opposite effect.

Maurice thought *That bastard coming up here to appoligize, he just wants to look like he's so damned noble in front of his damned preacher and he'll be telling everyone he sees It's a wonder that he didn't bring a reporter with him. That damnbed kiss ass junk yard dog.*

Jack told Missie how things turned out.

"I should have gone with you. I could have told that lap dog what little green apples are made of and I would've given him a dose of his own medicine. And it would have given me a chance to call him lap dog again So he looked bad did he? That makes me feel good. I wonder how his stupid deputy looks." Missie said

GOOD NIGHT

That night when Jack got ready for bed he knelt in prayer as was his custom. It was a habit that Mable had instilled in him long before he had any idea of who God was. Although he still wondered about that. He knows who Jesus is and Jesus was the one that provided him a way to God. He knows from experience that there is a merciful God that takes care of things. When he prayed he asked to be forgiven for the part he played in shaping Maurice's mind to make him so bitter and he asked God to forgive Maurice. Then he thought again, "Oh yes, God I forgive the Reverend Mathews also. I also ask for your forgiveness for all the hate I've harbored in my heart for so long."

After Jack had truly forgiven everyone he had held a grudge against he found that it really was a blessing. He no longer would bring to mind the terrible or unpleasant things and realized that his hatred for anyone only made him relive the moments. He lived a peaceful and pleasant life.

Would you like to see your manuscript become a book?

If you are interested in becoming a PublishAmerica author, please submit your manuscript for possible publication to us at:

acquisitions@publishamerica.com

You may also mail in your manuscript to:

**PublishAmerica
PO Box 151
Frederick, MD 21705**

www.publishamerica.com

CPSIA information can be obtained at www.ICGtesting.com
Printed in the USA
240869LV00001B/44/P